SOUTHERN STAR

SOUTHERN STAR

•

Phyllis Humphrey and Carolann Camillo

AVALON BOOKS
NEW YORK

Library of Congress Cataloging-in-Publication Data

Humphrey, Phyllis A.
    Southern Star / Phyllis Humphrey and Carolann Camillo.
        p. cm.
    ISBN 978-0-8034-7705-6 (acid-free paper)   1. Yachting—
Fiction.   2. Love stories.   I. Camillo, Carolann.   II. Title.
    PS3608.U474S68 2010
    813'.6—dc22

                                                2010022418

PRINTED IN THE UNITED STATES OF AMERICA
ON ACID-FREE PAPER
BY HADDON CRAFTSMEN, BLOOMSBURG, PENNSYLVANIA

To our husbands, who don't think
we're crazy when we spend hours
at our computers creating alternate lives

Acknowledgments

Thanks to the late Mona Schreiber, who introduced us in her writing class, and to everyone in our critique groups who offered their insight and encouragement over the years.

Chapter One

I wouldn't ask Gary Pritchard to captain *Southern Star* if he were the last skipper left alive in the Bahamas!"

Marilee Shaw rarely put herself in the position of having to eat her own words, but as she walked quickly along the dock to where the *Southern Star* lay tied at anchor, the challenge she'd uttered earlier lingered in her ears as well as on her tongue. So much for rash promises.

"That sounds vaguely familiar, except this morning it was the entire world." Jane Owens, who owned a catering service that supplied food for local charters, and who at sixty had the energy of most women at forty-five, hurried to keep up with Marilee's long-legged stride. "Now that you've changed your mind, let's not quibble over geography."

As she neared the yacht she had recently inherited, Marilee slowed her pace. The largest and most luxurious of the two dozen craft berthed in the marina, the *Star* swayed gently atop the water's surface.

"I wish I could think of one good reason, even two

bad ones, why he should agree to take the *Southern Star* out on this cruise." Her gaze swept the fifty-two-foot length of the yacht. With a sigh, she climbed the gangplank, a red-and-white FOR SALE sign in one hand and a roll of tape in the other. Although the *Star* was listed with three brokers—one at Harbour Island on Eleuthera and two in Nassau, the capital of the Bahamas—it paid to be practical.

"He loved you once," Jane said from the deck below. "Men don't forget those things, although they like to pretend they do."

"Whatever he felt, that was eight years ago. Men don't stay in love that long." All he was likely to remember was how much she'd hurt him. "He'll say no."

After securing the sign to the forward window of the saloon, Marilee turned quickly and, with Jane, left the yacht and dock behind, heading for the nearby cinder block building that housed her late father's South Wind Charters office. As she made her way across the asphalt roadway and down the cement sidewalk, a crisp Atlantic breeze carrying the fresh, clean scent of salt air riffled through her hair. The sun felt warm on her skin, and she would have liked to enjoy it further, but enjoyment of any kind had been pushed to somewhere below "read everything by Shakespeare" on her list of priorities.

She pushed open the office door and went to the desk where piles of invoices, outdated correspondence, and an unhealthy preponderance of bills greeted her. Having sorted through all that paper for the past three weeks, she wanted to sweep it into the trash and return home to California.

"I need a miracle," she said. "Only something tells me that Gary will not be the knight who rides to my rescue."

"Then why are you going all the way down to Governor's Harbour when you already know his answer?" Mischief danced in the depths of Jane's dark eyes.

"Because I'm a masochist." Marilee sank into the ancient swivel chair. "Because I have this overpowering urge to have him slam the door in my face. Because I believe in living dangerously. Take your pick."

"I like the last," Jane said.

"Unfortunately, I have few options. This is simple economics. Either I honor the last commitment Dad left on the books, or the bank will repossess the *Star.*" She stared at the invoice confirming a ten-day charter for Tom Wellman and a party of four. The very fact of the cruise seemed an answer to her prayers. How else could she make even one payment to the bank?

"Dad put his entire life into the *Star,*" she continued. "Now he's left her to me, every gleaming, mortgaged foot of her. They'll sell her at auction for a fraction of what she's worth. I can't let them do that."

"You've convinced me," Jane said, "and you'll convince Gary. I think it a good sign he's come back to Eleuthera after all those years he lived away. As if he knew you were going to need him."

"That's one way of looking at it." Marilee had already decided she needed a second miracle—finding a skipper. She stood and picked up her keys. "But I still wish there was another way. *Any* other way. Taming lions would have to be a picnic compared to coaxing Gary into this assignment."

She remembered their last meeting vividly. Hurt had burned in his eyes, and it had taken her the better part of two years to stop hating herself for what she believed, at the time, was the right decision.

"Don't feel you have to be overly scrupulous." Jane, never one to keep good advice to herself, pressed each point home with emphasis. "Play on his sense of fairness. Your father helped Gary get started in this business, made it possible for him to buy his first yacht. Loyalty and obligation are sentiments he'll understand."

"I'll try." Marilee paused at the door. "But will they work when he knows I've got a fifty-two-foot white elephant on my hands?"

"Gary Pritchard was like a son to your father. You might want to remind him of that too."

They stepped out into the bright sunshine. "This sounds like a pep rally. You know, one up for our side." She laughed, but it came out sounding forced.

After saying good-bye to Jane, she climbed into the Jeep. As she turned the key, its engine sprang to life. She felt a moment's hesitation, but before she allowed herself to think of the consequences, she swung the Jeep onto the road and headed south toward Governor's Harbour.

Her memory was good and the area she sought was not too difficult to find. Eleuthera Island, less than one hundred miles long and under five miles wide in many places, could be covered in less than three hours. In the past, she had explored every inch of it with her father, but that had been only after her parents divorced and he moved from Florida to the Bahamas, where he thought business would be better. She drove past old homes, lying on either side of the hill, half secluded by tropical shrubs, tranquil and quiet. That day, however, she had no time to slow down and admire their quaint beauty. She went past the few shops, the supermarket, the bank, and the church she had once attended and over the ridge where the road ran toward sandy beaches.

An hour later, she recognized Gary's house from Jane's brief description. She climbed out of the Jeep and walked slowly up the flagstone path. All smoked glass and wood and vaulted roof, the house was bordered on three sides by immaculately kept emerald lawns. Just beyond, across an expanse of pink sand dotted with lush green palms, the ocean rushed at the shore. In a swirl of sparkling turquoise, it inched up onto the beach only to be swept back out to sea. Almost mesmerized by the motion of the water, ebbing and flowing, rising on a high, sweet crest, only to crash and slip away, she realized her relationship with Gary had been like that.

If it was possible to love a man too much, to become totally captivated by the sight and sound of him, then that was how she had loved Gary Pritchard. But what she had felt for him in the beginning had become, at the end, too strong, too consuming, so that when he asked her to marry him, she knew without a moment's doubt that she could never share him with his mistress, the sea. She could never have become a part-time fixture in his life . . . like her mother had been in her father's.

She pushed the bell. A chime sounded somewhere in the interior of the house, soft and muted. It died and she waited, finally deciding, almost with a sense of relief, that no one was home. Before she had a chance to consider what plan to adopt next—leaving a note was out of the question—something furry brushed against her. With a small gasp, she looked down to find a fat orange- and white-striped cat looking up at her.

"Where did you come from?" she said aloud.

The cat examined Marilee, then strolled languorously to the door, where it stretched its front paws against the polished mahogany.

Surprised to find so tame an animal on the premises— a pair of Great Danes would have seemed more appropriate for the Gary Pritchard she remembered—Marilee said, "Don't tell me you belong here!"

"He doesn't. I gave him a handout once or twice and I haven't been able to get rid of him since. I call him Cat."

The voice that came from directly behind Marilee was low and husky, familiar, and intensely masculine, like its owner. She straightened up and turned in that direction.

"Lee."

Except for the deeper lines etched into his brow and along the sides of his mouth, he had, in her view, changed very little. At thirty-two, he was still slim where it counted, the muscles finely toned in his long legs and upper arms. Dark hair fell carelessly in thick waves to frame his face, and his blue eyes were exactly as she remembered them, alive with a curiosity and zest for living that had once made him the most exciting man she had ever met.

"Hello, Gary." Her heartbeat shifted into high gear.

She took a series of deep breaths. In, out, in, out, like a do-it-yourself mouth-to-mouth resuscitation.

He took a half step toward her, then drew back. "Well." He sounded uncertain, which heightened Marilee's own nervousness.

"How are you, Gary?" There, she had managed to say his name twice without sounding like a breathy ingenue.

"Right this minute, surprised would be an understatement." After a moment, the uncertainty disappeared from his voice. "You look wonderful, Lee."

"You look well too." It was her turn to understate. Dressed in denim cutoffs and navy blue tank top, he looked as vital, tanned, and handsome as ever.

"I had no idea you were here on Eleuthera." A tiny smile flirted with the corners of his lips.

"I'm on temporary leave from my job." The cat brushed against Marilee, then leaped to its adopted owner, rubbing against his legs.

"Computers, isn't it?"

"Yes." Had her father told him that? Or had he asked about her? She wondered what else he knew about her life. "I'm with Visions Unlimited. I help businesses develop networking systems, use new software."

"You're a teacher. That's a good career for you, Lee."

"What makes you say that?" She laughed. "Have you pictured me as some outdated stereotype of a teacher, in stout shoes and frumpy dress, my hair pulled into a bun?"

"Hardly. And it would be a shame to hide that hair."

His smile softened his rugged features. "But it's conservative and predictable."

"Not the kind of work I do." She felt an urge to defend herself. "My territory takes in three states. I could be in San Diego one day and Seattle the next. There are times I have to catch a flight on less than four hours' notice. It's hectic, but it is *not* predictable."

"I'm glad." He smiled more broadly this time. "You've changed, then. That's good."

Oh, he was going to make this very difficult. Why had she allowed herself to hope otherwise? "I have less than a month left to sort out Dad's affairs. The business is in terrible shape. I . . . I suppose you heard."

He nodded, genuine sorrow flicking to the surface of his eyes. "I'm sorry, Lee. He was a good friend—the best—and I'll miss him. I was in Miami when he died. I didn't find out about it until last week."

He pushed open the door and reached toward her.

Her first instinct was to back away, but before she could act on the impulse, his long fingers brushed her arm. With the slightest pressure, he guided her into the cool interior of the house.

"I appreciate your driving all this way to tell me."

Guilt washed over her momentarily, and she followed him into a large living room, but its simple beauty failed to register on her. Rattan chairs, glass-topped tables, recessed lighting, and a woven straw rug made only fleeting impressions. Her conscious mind was filled with the man, not his surroundings, and also of the fact that she was disturbed he could still have such an effect on her. On the drive down to his house, she felt convinced she had made peace with herself over Gary. Now, she wasn't so sure.

"Can I get you something? Club soda or coffee? I'm afraid that's all I can offer you just now."

She shook her head. How could she admit she had come, not to share her grief with him, but to offer him a proposition, yacht owner to yacht owner? That she had, in essence, materialized on his doorstep to offer him a job?

"Gary . . . I . . ." She turned toward the tall sheets of glass that formed the side wall of the room. "I like your view." She wished again that she didn't need his help.

"I like the one I'm looking at." He came up behind her, and she felt vulnerable again. She wished she hadn't come rushing down there wearing her yellow terry cloth shorts and top, as if she were still eighteen. Brief hot-weather clothes were usually all she had ever worn when she visited her father. But now, at twenty-six, their encounter was to be strictly business. Had to be. But with the mere sight of him warming her face and turning her hands clammy, surely that was wishful thinking.

Chapter Two

Marilee turned away from the sea to face Gary. A nervous smile that must have looked like a half-grimace crossed her face, precipitating more deep breathing.

"Lee, are you feeling well? I really think I'd better get you something cool to drink."

"Maybe a glass of water," she conceded, following him into the kitchen.

He pulled open the refrigerator door to reveal a package of cheese, a half loaf of bread, some eggs, and an assortment of canned drinks. She peered at the nearly empty shelves.

"I see some things about you haven't changed. You must still eat on the run." The paucity of food—forget nourishing—she could reconcile with the man she used to know. But this room . . . Her eyes swept the enormous space that housed a double oven, acres of cabinets, racks of copper pots and pans, and a center island of gleaming stainless steel that might have been a prop in *Star Wars*. "This room is crying out for Julia Child."

He laughed. "Do you think I overdid it? I do cook a little, but I haven't shopped lately."

"You could cater banquets from here." She wondered if he cooked "a little" for a special woman. In fact, he might have built the house with her in mind, someone who could tolerate the long separations when he was out on a cruise. There must be women like that somewhere. Perhaps his obvious success and the income that provided this upscale property was compensation enough for them. She dismissed the thought. Whom Gary saw and how they responded to his here-today, gone-tomorrow ways no longer interested her.

"Lee?"

She dragged her thoughts back to the present to find him offering her a glass of sparkling soda. She recognized the glass at once and her heart did a sort of leap.

"You still have these?"

He flashed a smile. "Fine crystal like this? Did you think I'd let anything happen to them?"

The glasses were tall and narrow, with Disney characters etched on the front in living color. She remembered there had been a set of eight. They came as part of the furnishings when he had bought his own charter yacht, the *Seafarer*.

"You wanted to toss them overboard." She took the Mickey Mouse glass from him.

"You insisted I keep them."

"I'm glad you did," she said, her throat tight. "I still like them." She remembered how she had made him promise to use the glasses after she returned to school in Florida. It seemed one way to ensure his thinking about her, although at the time she was only fifteen and he a very much older, very much more sophisticated twenty-one.

"What shall we drink to?" His voice turned low and soft.

Marilee shook her head, her hair swinging in accompaniment to her loss for words. The afternoon was not going at all as she had expected. Why had he not shown the slightest sign of resentment?

"How about to old times and old . . . friends?" he said, clicking her glass with his Donald Duck one. He sipped at his drink while she stared solemnly into the clear liquid in her own.

"Lee, why haven't you married?"

The question caught her totally off guard. He seemed to know a lot about her. "I . . . I'm waiting for the right man." Her response must have sounded completely inane to him, but what had he hoped: that she would confess to having made the wrong decision eight years before when she turned down his proposal?

"And you haven't found him yet?" His tone was surprisingly gentle.

"There is someone. I'm not sure." She hadn't intended to give him an opening, but there it was anyway.

"What are you afraid of? Making a mistake, or committing yourself to a man?"

She drew back from him. "I'm not afraid of anything," she managed calmly, "and certainly not of committing myself to a man. Only the wrong one."

"And this, what's-his-name, isn't. Maybe."

"His name is Howard."

"Howard." He smiled. "He sounds like an account-ant." There was a Hugh Jackman smoothness to his tone.

"He's a lawyer," she said evenly. "I know that's far too conventional for your taste, but he's very success-ful. Very good at what he does."

"And you only think you love him?" For a moment his guard dropped, and those ice-blue eyes impaled her own. If he expected her to flinch, he had a major disap-pointment coming. She'd been right earlier. The mantle of civility sat uneasily on his shoulders, and for a man like Gary, who never engaged in petty personality games, she had to give him credit for keeping up the pretense that long.

"Gary, I didn't drive half the length of Eleuthera to discuss my private life." She sensed that the moment to confront him about the *Southern Star* and its mortgage had come, and she couldn't afford lost chances. Even if they rested with a man who probably despised her. "In fact, I have somewhat of a confession to make."

"A confession? That sounds ominous."

She watched his expression soften and observed his metamorphosis back to gracious host.

"Let me guess," he said, refilling her glass. "You did not come down here to tell me about your father."

The moment of truth approached. As she watched him from across the room, she hoped he would put aside his resentment of her at least long enough to skipper what would, most likely, be the *Star*'s last cruise.

"Nor, I'm willing to bet, was it my fatal charm draw-ing you like a magnet." He drained his glass and set it down onto a spotless granite countertop.

"Or was it?" He moved quickly, cutting the space between them in half. She attempted a retreat, yet somehow remained rooted to the spot, as if someone had poured a magnum of cement into her canvas deck shoes.

"No." The word, almost a whisper, seemed in direct contradiction to her answer. Goodness, she was making a mess of this.

"No," she said again, regaining her voice and her equilibrium. She stepped away from him again before his nearness could remind her of the past.

"This is business, Gary. I came to see you about the *Southern Star.*" She let her gaze be drawn into the deep well of his eyes, to reaffirm to herself and him that he could no longer affect her emotions.

"The *Star,*" he echoed softly.

"Dad left her to me, but there are problems. I'm going to lose her. She's mortgaged right up to here." She raised her hand to eye level. "And unless I do something quickly, the bank will take possession of her next month."

A serious expression crossed his face. "Let's talk in the living room. It's more comfortable there."

After gesturing Marilee toward a chair, he settled into a nest of green pillows in an opposite corner of the couch. The cat leaped into his lap.

"So, are you in business, Lee? With the *Star?*"

"That, I suppose, depends entirely on you."

"Me?" If finding her on his doorstep, washed up by the tide as it were, had caught him by surprise, then her declaration seemed to have no less an effect.

"There's a confirmation for a ten-day cruise on the

men at the marina who've had experience with large yachts."

"I don't want those young men to crew." He spoke softly, and she could see a new expression flicker in those vivid blue eyes. The moment of truth.

"Well, of course, you're free to hire anyone."

"I want you."

She had guessed correctly after all. Gary would have his revenge in his own way and in his own time. She turned away from him to stare, unseeing, out the window. Her voice faltered momentarily, then her temper flared. She shook her head.

"I don't think that would be a very good idea. For one thing—"

"I'm not asking you, Lee. It's that or find yourself another skipper." He paused. "That shouldn't be too much of a sacrifice for you. I was under the impression you were willing to do anything to save the *Star.*"

He had come up behind her and, seeing his reflection in the glass, she swung around to face him again. "I am, except . . ."

"Except what? You don't want to dirty your hands?" He swung his head slowly from side to side, a sly grin on his face. "I'm disappointed in you, Lee."

"I have nothing against hard work," she protested. "If necessary I can cook, serve meals, clean up, do laundry, drop anchor, and sort fishing gear. But I don't think it's a good idea for us to be together in such close quarters on the *Star* for ten days."

His hearty laugh echoed in the high-ceilinged room. "Close quarters? Is that what's bothering you?" Merri-

books, and I had hoped to go ahead with it." She watched him across what appeared to be an acre of glass-topped coffee table.

"I need a captain, Gary. Someone local who knows the waters and won't run the *Star* onto a reef. I need someone reliable and experienced and I need him now."

"I take it you didn't come here for a recommendation."

"I'll be honest," she continued, wanting to get the whole thing into the open quickly. "I phoned every captain within a radius of fifty miles, but they were all booked. You're my last resort."

She had the good grace to wince at the gaffe. He seemed not in the least perturbed.

"The accountant, I gather, is out of the question. Wouldn't know anything about the sea?"

"What accountant?" He was talking in riddles.

"Howard."

Gary was clearly the most irritating, aggravating, infuriating man in all the Bahamas. No, she had been right earlier, in all the world.

"He's a lawyer. I told you that." She wondered why he had brought Howard into the conversation. Did it upset Gary to think she had a romantic interest in her life?

"Whatever."

She refused to be put off. "Jane told me you hadn't used her catering service since you moved back to Eleuthera and built this house. So I took that as a hopeful sign you didn't have a cruise booked for the *Sea-farer* in the immediate future. I'm the first to admit this is presumptuous, but who knows better than you what the *Star* meant to my dad?"

On a roll now, she decided to take Jane's advice and appeal to his sense of loyalty.

"You worked alongside him enough years to understand that. But you also know how impractical he could be. I've tried everything to avoid repossession, from pressuring Mike and the other yacht brokers to find a buyer to coming close to groveling on my knees at the bank."

She pressed this home with a wan smile. "That's why I need this cruise. With the money I can earn, less expenses, of course—I intend to pay the going rate for a captain—I can make an additional payment or two on the mortgage while the brokers try to sell her."

She finished with a rush of breath, convinced she hadn't done the most credible job. He couldn't miss the irony of the situation. Eight years before, she had refused to marry him because of the way he made his living. Now she was trying to hire him to do that very thing for her. He would have to refuse.

He removed the cat from his lap, pulled his feet off the coffee table, and stood. "I don't know what the going rate is these days, Lee, but whatever it is, you've got yourself a skipper. Provided we can work out the details." He moved toward her and held out his hand.

She looked up at him, her mouth agape, as if he had just said he was booked on the next space shuttle.

"I do?" She felt the strength in his hand as it closed over hers, and she came to her feet.

"You seem surprised." He continued to hold her hand in his. Success or not, the sight of him, the feel of his hand, made her wonder if this had really been a good idea.

"Did you think I'd let those bad men down at the bank foreclose on the old homestead—excuse me, yacht? No when I know how much she means to you."

There was nothing overtly sarcastic in his tone, but it disturbed her nonetheless.

And what did he know about it, anyway? Her earliest memories were of the *Southern Star:* sitting in her father's lap, pretending to take the wheel, climbing over the side for her first swimming lesson, being rocked to sleep by the rhythms of the sea. In later years she never thought of the *Star* without a tugging in her heart. It was where, at thirteen, she had met Gary Pritchard, and where, five years later, she had fallen deeply in love with him.

She disengaged her hand and stepped around him to walk toward the window overlooking the beach. Let him make snide remarks if he must. She supposed he was entitled to them, although she wasn't at all sure he hadn't had more than his quota already. And what did she care about anything concerning Gary anymore except that he had agreed to her proposal?

She swung around to face him again. "I'm very relieved, and grateful." In the back of her mind a nagging suspicion surfaced that everything had gone too smoothly. But why, she admonished herself, ruin a perfectly delectable moment of triumph by admitting a niggling, possibly nonexistent, doubt?

"I've spoken to Jane about the catering. Just in case she added hastily, not wanting him to think she had taken his acceptance for granted. "So it's only a matter of hiring someone to crew. There are a couple of you

ment danced in the depths of his eyes in contrast to the innocent mask that guarded his face. "There are two crew staterooms in the bow. One for you, one for me. What did you think I meant?" He closed the space between them and looped his finger around the stray lock of hair that had fallen against her cheek, tucking it behind her ear.

"And with four other people on board, we'll be well chaperoned. So there's no reason for you to run away and hide again."

His words shattered the intimacy of the moment, an intimacy she realized too late that he had deliberately and calculatedly built in order to coax a response from her. His overly friendly manner, his laughter and gentleness didn't fool her one bit. He was intent on making her miserable any way he could, so she had better watch out. If one thing hadn't been completely clear earlier, it was now. Vengeance must have an all-too-sweet taste for him. And no wonder. He had waited eight long years for it.

"I'm not running away, Gary, and I no longer have any need to hide from you." Her tone was strained, but the words came out crisp enough.

He smiled. "Good." He paused. "We once worked very well together, remember? Do you think you can do that again?"

"To save the *Star?* Yes, I can." Yet she knew that those ten days were going to be the most trying days of her life. He would probably take every opportunity to remind her of a past that she was slowly, consciously coming to realize was anything but dead. A past she'd hoped he had reconciled with . . . but apparently not.

Her gaze swept over the contours of his face, studied the perfect nose, straight lips, the intensity in his blue eyes. Yes, it was entirely possible hard feelings remained. And why not? He was human. Or—and she would have to give this some thought later—could it be that he still felt some remnant of the love he had once confessed to her? Probably not, her instinct told her. It was true he had loved her once, but a man like Gary Pritchard carried no eight-year torches.

"So, I take it we're partners in this little venture?"

"Oh, yes," she said, her voice taking on an unmistakable firmness. She must not let him intimidate her. It was imperative that, from the start, she stand up to him.

"I'll call you tonight to give you all the particulars." She made her way to the front door.

"That won't be necessary." He held the door open for her. "I'll be up your way tomorrow, early. We can discuss all the particulars then."

Not answering, she headed for the Jeep. Nevertheless, she felt certain she'd won the first round. The *Star* had a captain. But as she pulled away from his house, she couldn't help wondering if it was a victory after all.

Chapter Three

Marilee opened her eyes the next morning to pools of sunlight dancing on the cabin ceiling. Beyond the open porthole window, a cloudless sky stretched toward the far-off horizon, heralding another clear, hot day.

Memories rushed in on the faint morning breeze—memories of living, every day until she was eight, on Eleuthera. In the intervening years, after she and her mother moved to California, only the summers—and not every one at that—brought her back to visit her father and the islands they both loved.

Pushing aside the soft white sheet, she sat up in one of the two double beds that occupied a third of the master stateroom, the larger of the two situated in the stern of the ship. The clock that sat on a metal foot locker beside the bed showed the time to be just after nine, at least an hour later than she had been used to waking. Not surprisingly, she'd slept fitfully the night before and even dreamed of her fateful reunion with Gary Pritchard.

She stepped out of bed to tropical heat. An early dip

held great appeal, but since swimming was not allowed in the boat docking area, she settled for a shower in the cubicle adjacent to the stateroom. The cool water revived her and, after toweling dry and slipping into a yellow tank top and white shorts, she entered the galley. Compact and built only for quick meals, everything in it was well within reach. She filled the automatic coffeemaker with water and, while waiting for it to drip through the filter, ate an orange and popped two blueberry muffins into the microwave oven.

A few minutes later, she ascended the steps toward the saloon. Setting down the plate with the muffins, she pushed open the hatch and stepped out onto the deck. The glare of the sun momentarily blinding her, she paused to adjust her eyes. Then a voice, unexpectedly close, startled her. She spun her head around toward the dock.

"Permission to come aboard?"

The masculine tone left no doubt as to its owner. Had her dream been accompanied by sound, the man who haunted it would have spoken in exactly that tone. Although she resented his toying with her the day before, there was a sudden increased tempo in her heart-beat, the result, she told herself, of the suddenness of his appearance and not because of any attraction to the man himself.

"Permission granted." The moment she spoke the words they puzzled her. How effortlessly she had replied to the once-familiar request. She guessed it was a reflex, something she had always done when she spent time there with her father so long ago. The only people who ever used that expression were friends and were always welcome. Strangers would say things like "Yoo-hoo" or "Hello, there" and state their business from the apparent safety of the dock instead of asking if they could board.

Gary stepped easily over the railing without bothering to lift it out of the way and strode across the deck of the *Southern Star* toward her. The green- and white-striped short-sleeved shirt he wore over white cotton trousers set off the deep tan of his arms and throat.

"Mmm, that coffee smells good." He stepped under the blue canvas canopy that covered the entire stern of the deck and settled himself into a navy blue canvas director's chair. There was nothing in his attitude to suggest they had parted the day before on less than cordial terms.

Wary and in no mood for any more surprises—the previous day had held quite enough, thank you—Marilee set her mug down on the large plank table.

"Wouldn't you like to look around for a while? Refresh your memory?" She might have to spend the next ten days in close quarters with him, but there was nothing in their verbal contract that stipulated sharing her breakfast.

Gary appraised her looks before answering, his gaze skimming over her face.

"I have a very vivid memory. Maybe later. First, I'd love a cup of coffee. You don't mind if I join you?" His lips turned up in a teasing smile, and there was an unmistakable flash of warmth in his blue eyes.

Yes, in fact, she minded very much. Her instinct told her that lying beneath the surface of this innocuous little coffee break he'd instigated was the reminder that Captain Pritchard was very much in command of their little one-ship armada. If he asked her to fetch him a cup of coffee, he expected her to do it. So, okay, she would. Why quibble over a small disturbance when there were bound to be dangerous squalls on the horizon?

"One coffee coming up." She slipped down the ladder.

In the galley, she found another mug and poured his coffee. She remembered the muffins, decided it would be selfish—a trait she disliked—to eat both herself, and pulled another plate from the cupboard before rejoining him.

He was sitting at an angle, his back leaning into the corner of the chair, one leg crossed casually over the other. He hadn't yet become aware of her approach, and she found herself stopping just at the point where her eyes cleared the deck. A swell of emotion, of the kind long since put to rest where Gary was concerned, swept through her. It might have been eight years before, and whether reflex or memory had caused it, it was there, and it was as familiar as it was unwanted. But then again, when had she not been affected by him? Suddenly it passed, and she continued up onto the deck.

"I suppose you're hungry too." She set a plate and mug down on the table, slipped into the deck chair opposite him, and brought her mug to her lips with both hands. She didn't trust herself to say more at the moment. She'd asked the favor, and he had agreed. What she hadn't asked for was her totally unexpected and unwelcome reaction to the man.

When she next looked up at him over the rim of her mug, his blue eyes burned into hers.

"You're very quiet this morning. Did I upset you?" He leaned forward in his chair, his muscular arms resting on his knees. "After I agreed to bail you out, I would have thought you'd show a little enthusiasm, perhaps even a bit of gratitude at my decision." With this last statement, a spark of humor lit his eyes.

Was he playing cat to her mouse again this morning? "You know I'm grateful. I appreciate your cooperation. But if you expect me to throw myself into your arms because of it, you're very mistaken."

The lines at the corners of his eyes crinkled, and his lips curved into a smile. "If I ever find you in my arms, I hope it won't be through a sense of gratitude."

As she started to protest, he quickly added, "However, that's not what I expect. As long as we're working together, let's be professional, shall we?"

"I think that's the best way to handle the situation," she said. "After all, this is probably the only occasion we'll be required to work together."

Draining his coffee and setting the mug down on the table, Gary rose from the chair and stood before her. "Very good. Let's make preparations then. We need to get moving."

He strode to the doors of the saloon and went through them, ducking his head as he did so. Marilee jumped up and followed. Inside the saloon he could stand upright, and he pulled the FOR SALE sign from the window.

"I think we can do without this floating want ad." He

dropped the cardboard into a wicker wastebasket. Then he continued walking to the galley and down another few steps into the engine room, stooping each time to keep from banging his head on the low beams of the ladders.

Marilee followed a few paces behind, watching as he examined the engines, the fittings, and the valves, and checked the gauges for the two diesel fuel tanks. After pronouncing everything to be in order, he turned and they mounted the steps to the galley.

He opened cupboards at random, looked in the tiny re-frigerator, inspected the stainless steel sink, and assessed the narrow pantry. Then he folded his arms across his chest and gazed long and intently at her.

"I trust you've learned how to cook, Lee. The last I remember, your specialty was cheese sandwiches."

"I might never win the Pillsbury Bake-Off," she an-swered, "but I do well enough at it, considering my kitchen would fit nicely inside yours and still leave room for a Roller Derby." She paused. "Anyway, Jane will cater the food, and we'll store it in the freezer in the engine room. So all I'll have to do is heat the meals and serve them. I can handle breakfast and the occasional cold lunch. I know the routine. There'll be no complaints."

"Good." He lingered a moment, as if wanting to make another comment, then apparently thought better of it and left the galley to make his way to the forward cabin. She had to run to keep up with his long strides, follow-ing him inside the small space that served as the crew's quarters.

They were two tiny triangular-shaped rooms, with

narrow bunks along the walls and little cupboards beneath to store belongings. A narrow door led to a tiny toilet and shower room. Marilee, inspecting the facility, tripped over the raised threshold of the door, forgetting it was there.

"Careful." Gary took her gently by the arm. "Don't hurt yourself."

He leaned one open palm against the bulkhead. His closeness sent a shiver along her spine, a reminder of the effect he still had on her. "I like the thought of sailing with you again. Do you remember that day on the *Seafarer?*"

Remember? How could she ever forget? It was the first time, as an adult, she had ever been completely alone with him for any extended length of time. He had invited her to spend the day with him, cruising the waters off the coast of Spanish Wells aboard his newly purchased and, as he liked to joke, borrowed-from-the-bank yacht.

Marilee had been nervous, frightened by the intensity of her mounting feelings toward him, but even more afraid of his toward her. Although he had never touched her with any sense of intimacy, the looks they had exchanged that summer she was eighteen would have suggested, even to a stranger, that there was a powerful attraction growing between them.

As the cruise began, she could have asked nothing more of the day. A brilliant sun hung beneath a splash of cobalt blue sky, the tropical sea was calm and refreshing, and she enjoyed the exciting company of the man with whom she was falling in love. Was this merely a schoolgirl crush, or had she passed through that stage previously when her brief visits to her father had initially brought her into contact with Gary? Nevertheless, what she felt then, she was certain, she could never feel for another man.

Although everything appeared perfect, a strange tension built as the day progressed and totally disarmed her. Having only dated boys her own age, she was all too aware that Gary, at twenty-four, was far removed from the stage of playing boyish games. He had spent two of his college years in England, a fact which made him seem more articulate and even more mature. When he kissed her, and she knew without a doubt that he would, there would be nothing tentative in his kiss, nothing hesitant in his touch. How would she handle it? The mere thought of it thrilled her and, at the same time, worried her.

The ambivalence put a strain on her, and by late afternoon she had developed a throbbing headache. Blaming it on too much sun, she insisted that a few minutes' rest below would be enough. Leaving him on the rear deck, she made her way below to the stern and entered what she thought was the guest stateroom and lay down on the double bed. Closing her eyes, she gave herself up to the gentle rocking motion of the ship. In a while she dozed, and when she opened her eyes again, he was next to her, looking down.

"I was worried about you." He sat on the edge of the bed. With the backs of his fingers, he brushed the hair from her forehead. "Are you feeling any better?"

She tried to lift her head, but a dull ache sent her back onto the pillow.

"You're too tense," he whispered, leaning over her. "Try to relax." His thumbs drew circles against her temples. She started to speak, but she was silenced by Gary's descending mouth as he kissed her.

Her first instinct was to draw away, but the pressure on her mouth increased. Her two selves waged a silent battle, then her caution wavered, and she brought her arms around his neck.

Breaking the kiss, his voice a whisper, he said, "Let me love you, Lee."

His words provoked her earlier fears and, suddenly, she froze in his arms. The moment was spent as quickly as it had sprung to life. "What are you doing?"

He looked different somehow. Conflicting emotions seemed to wage a battle for his expression. Finally, in a husky voice that she could barely hear, he said, "I love you. I want us to spend our lives together."

These were words her teenage fantasies had imagined him saying. Yet, now that the moment had arrived, they failed to have the same effect. When she looked into his eyes, they showed a love stronger than any she might ever have dreamed of seeing. He was everything she wanted, everything she knew she could never have.

Anger and youthful inexperience took possession of her emotions. Fear came next. Although she loved seeing him every summer, their relationship exciting and romantic, she suddenly wondered if all that would change if she married him. In fact, she knew it would. His very profession made him a poor risk as a husband. Only too well had she learned the lesson of her parents' failed marriage. She remembered seeing her mother sitting alone day after day while her father took glamorous and wealthy people on deep-sea fishing trips. She wouldn't repeat that mistake. She couldn't.

"No, I won't marry you," she told him, her voice bold, the words sounding harsher than she expected, almost like a stinging rebuke.

He took it that way. He leaped from her side as if she had struck him, stared down at her for a long moment, and narrowed his eyes into dark slits.

"I never took you for a tease, or liar, or a coward. But I was wrong." He took several deep breaths, and then his voice dropped again. "It's my own fault. I should have known better."

He stormed out of the stateroom and turned the *Sea-farer* back toward Eleuthera. He did not speak to her again that summer. In September she started college, and the next summer she learned he had taken his yacht and moved off the island. Having parted after the scene on the yacht, Marilee had thought their separation would last forever.

Now her eyes met those of the man she had run from so long ago. Still affected by the brief reverie, she said, "There's nothing wrong with my memory." She wished there were, that she had not recalled that day, that moment in his arms, his words, her answer.

She should never have asked him to skipper the *Star* for the Wellmans' cruise, but it was too late to back out now.

Chapter Four

Marilee tried to brush past Gary, who was effectively blocking the door. "But I also recall we settled this question yesterday." She was annoyed with him now, for summoning up the past and, for, however half-heartedly, suggesting they might want to pick up where they had left off, only with a different ending.

He planted his strong hands on her shoulders. "Don't take everything so seriously, Lee. Whatever you think, I'm still a gentleman."

Without waiting for a comment, he released his hold and, entering one of the tiny staterooms, pushed up the hatch in the ceiling. Then, while stepping on the side of the bunk, he boosted himself up through the opening and went out on the deck. Marilee tried to follow, although somewhat awkwardly, and at the last moment Gary had to take her by the arms and pull her through. It brought them close, but her expression made it clear she would brook no intimacy and he let her go.

"Thanks for the help, but don't expect anything like that to happen again."

He threw back his head and laughed. "You've got fire, Lee. I'll give you that. I'll have to beware or you may mutiny before the cruise even begins."

He strode away from her again, walking the length of the deck toward the saloon and then descending the stairs into the room once more and down the right-hand ladder, this time into the passageway leading to the two staterooms. Once again Marilee was right behind him, mindful she had left her bed unmade and her belongings strewn about. It did not go unnoticed.

He picked up her nightgown that was little more than a violet and beige wisp of fabric and let it dangle from one finger. "I run a tidy ship, mate. There's a place for everything and . . ."

". . . everything in its place." Marilee snatched the garment away from him, folded it neatly, and tucked it under the pillow. In short order, sandals, shorts, swimsuit, and the pale-pink slacks she'd worn the night before were in their proper compartments.

Meanwhile, Gary continued his inspection, nodding with satisfaction at the double beds, the built-in chests of drawers, the closets. "How's the linen supply?" he asked next. "You'll need several changes of sheets and towels, unless you intend to wash frequently."

Marilee refused to be goaded. "I've already told you I'm prepared to handle that. In between cooking, cleaning, crewing, and general slaving, I expect to beat them against the rocks!"

He faced her in the narrow space between the beds,

his previous amusement turning in a moment to something else, perhaps a bitter memory. He seized her hands and held them in a tight grip. "There are still many countries around the world where the women do exactly that. And they do it willingly, patiently, and uncomplainingly. I suspect that leaves neither the time nor the energy for sarcasm when they go home to their husbands."

Marilee's face burned with indignation and she pulled her hands free. "You're not my husband."

The taunt was pure reflex, nothing she would ever have said consciously, and she regretted it immediately.

Pain and hurt flashed in his eyes, only to be replaced an instant later with nonchalance, as if he regretted letting her unsettle him. "You made that decision clear at the time." Then he shrugged, and his expression grew more serious. "My reference, however, was meant as a social commentary, not to dig up a past which has little meaning for either of us. I apologize."

There was an almost total lack of expression in his recital, leaving her to wonder which to believe—his apparent unconcern or the hurt she had seen earlier.

He eased by her and stopped at the door. "You can do the laundry anywhere—Tarpum Bay, Exuma, Nassau, wherever we happen to be at the time."

He left the master stateroom, then opened the door to the second. This was not much larger than the one Marilee would occupy, with two bunks staggered on top of one another, a built-in chest of drawers, and one porthole.

In a few strides he was up the ladder again, inspecting the saloon. Marilee followed, her gaze sweeping over the white leather lounges, the two swiveling easy chairs covered in a dark-blue print fabric, the dining table, lamps, shelves for books, and the portholes covered by short white drapes. The paneled walls gleamed with good care and gave a cozy atmosphere, and the blue carpeted floor silenced his footsteps when he moved quickly across the room.

"You might get some current magazines," he said. "These seem to be out of date."

They mounted the steps and this time, after inspecting the dinghy on the roof, went to the bridge, where he examined the wheel, checked gauges, and looked at the fuel supply. He opened the map drawers, from which he pulled sailing charts, and checked them rapidly.

"The navigation charts seem to be in order, but we'll need to get provisions. You can discuss that with Jane." He checked the fuel gauge. "She's almost full, but I'll have to see about topping off the tanks. I'll also check the spare parts and see to the first-aid kit. But first, we ought to take her out for a shake-down cruise."

"A shake-down cruise?"

"Yes, it's been many years since I piloted the *Star* and I'd like to get the feel of her again, learn how she responds. What do you say we take her out?"

"Now? Where? For how long?"

"Just for a couple of hours, around past Spanish Wells to Royal Island and back. I promise to get you home before dark, if that's what's worrying you."

"Why should that worry me?" she said casually, as if being alone with him on a tropical night was no cause for concern. "Anyway, do I have a choice?"

"Not really." He reached out to the table and picked up their untouched plates. "Here, eat this. You'll need something." He pushed one of the muffins at Marilee and descended once more through the open doors to the saloon, eating the other as he went.

Marilee threw herself into a chair and reflected in silence for a few minutes. She wanted desperately to call the whole thing off. How could she possibly live on the ship with him for ten days? In many ways he was the same Gary she had known before—handsome, flippant, masterful—but now there seemed to be an underlying current of intrigue, as if he were planning to turn the voyage to his advantage in more ways than earning a fee.

Even worse, her attitude when she was with him needed serious adjustment. She knew she had long since forgiven herself—and him—for the mistakes of the past. Her usual demeanor around others was that of a person of kindness and compassion. She knew she needed to be that way with Gary as well. She'd stop her belligerent behavior right now.

That settled, she realized she was famished, and the muffin looked delicious. As she ate, she thought of the long days stretching before her. She could do it, because, of course, she had to. She had known that the day before. It wasn't bad enough that the bank might sell the *Star* for a pittance, a situation that would make her father turn over in his grave. As the owner, she was still responsible for the loan and would be required to come up with any unpaid balance on the mortgage. Her savings account was nowhere near equal to that. To say nothing of the fact that she had to take her two months' leave without pay. That was why she had approached Gary Pritchard, of all people. Desperation.

Now that she had, she'd put up with him for ten days. She would put animosity behind her and work with him in a friendly manner. She would be cook, bottle-washer, and Girl Friday to his Robinson Crusoe. She had tackled tougher jobs before; she wasn't her father's daughter for nothing. On those short trips with her when she was a child, her father had been a stern taskmaster too, insisting that she perform her chores to the best of her ability, and she loved him for it. The discipline of the sailor's life was demanding, but also rewarding. If she had to work hard, at least she would enjoy the feel of the deck under her feet, the wind in her face, the beautiful sunrises and sunsets, the lush tropical islands with warm blue waters.

By the time she finished her muffin, she was resigned to her task and almost content. If it wasn't her father acting as captain, at least it was someone her own father had trained, and she could trust him to do a good job. He was certainly different from Howard.

Why had Howard crossed her mind just then? It was true she had hoped that two months away from him would finally help clarify her feelings about him, but since getting off the plane she'd hardly given him a moment's thought. It was as if she wanted to postpone any decision about Howard, not settle it. And now, to her consternation, she found herself comparing him with Gary.

He was not as tall as Gary, nor as handsome, but she had never cared much about the popular notions of good looks in people. Character was always more important to her. Why then did Gary's looks seem so appealing? She liked the way his thick, black hair grew low on his neck, and the intense blue of his eyes. And he was strong and capable. It always seemed to her that there was nothing Gary couldn't do if he put his mind or muscles to it.

But there was even more. Howard was intelligent, but Gary had matured in that direction as well. His manner of speaking, his choice of words, his confidence, all bespoke a person of much more than mere charm and ability.

Gary called to her, and, abandoning her thoughts about him, she quickly descended the ladder. For the next half hour she worked alongside him, helping him cast off the lines, maneuver the craft from its slip, and steer the *Southern Star* out of the harbor. With the engines running slowly, sailing at only five miles an hour, they were a long time leaving the harbor, but finally were into open water. The steady swish of the craft, the sunny day with puffy white clouds in a blue sky, made Marilee forget her earlier doubts. It would be a wonderful trip.

After an hour of sailing, Gary cut the engines and called to her. "How about a swim before lunch?"

She hesitated a moment, then agreed, and ducked down the ladder to the stateroom where she changed quickly into a green- and yellow-flowered swimsuit. She paused at the mirror on the wall and tied her hair back. The light tan color was already streaked with blond and would be more so, she knew, after ten days in the sun. That is, if she'd ever have more than a minute to be in the sun. She remembered the seemingly endless chores Gary had lined up for her.

Barefoot, she dashed up the steps and was on the deck in a moment. Without waiting for him, she dove into the water from the railing and came up several yards away from the *Star.* The water was cool and tingled on her skin, but heavenly, just the way she remembered it. She stroked easily away, enjoying the sensation of cool water and warm sun. She ducked down under the surface and swam for a few yards, her eyes adjusting to the underwater sights of tiny, darting fish, their bodies creating a kaleidoscope of gold and crimson, and far below, the dark blue depths. She came up, treading water, to look back at the beautiful sleek lines of the vessel that had now become hers.

And the bank's, she reminded herself.

She looked around and spotted Gary swimming near the stern of the ship. His wet hair glistened and his powerful tan shoulders and arms cut the surface as if he were captain of the entire Atlantic. He turned and spotted her watching him, then raised one arm in a wave. She had a sudden premonition that she, Gary, and the *Southern Star* were inescapably bound together, that they would play out a drama whose ending lay shrouded in mystery.

Immediately, she dismissed the notion as too much sun and shook her head. She would do this one last charter, sell the *Star*, and go back to California. Definitely.

Chapter Five

The Wellmans, the cruise customers her father had been expecting, weren't due for two days. Marilee used the first day to make arrangements with Jane for catering. Gary had announced he had things to handle before starting the ten-day excursion as well.

"Food for three meals a day for ten days for six people," Jane repeated when Marilee phoned her.

"I know that's a lot of work, but I'll help."

Jane chuckled. "You couldn't cook your way out of a pile of peeled potatoes."

"But I can do something," Marilee insisted.

"Yes, go shopping. But first get your skinny body over here so we can make a list of what we need."

Marilee had grinned at that. Jane liked to call her skinny because her curves weren't as ample as Jane's, but she knew she wasn't a pound under what the charts said were right for her height and body build.

So she'd gone to Jane's cottage, a whitewashed ranch-style house that served both as Jane's residence and business headquarters. She recognized the faded blue van Jane used for deliveries and parked the Jeep behind it. Then she followed the path around to the rear of the house, where the kitchen was located and where the tantalizing aroma of fresh-baked pastry hung in the air.

"You're just in time for a Scottish scone," Jane said.

"My timing is impeccable." Marilee's gaze swept over the extra-large kitchen, where a dozen pies were cooling on an oblong butcher block table that sat in the center of the room. Above the table, suspended from a rack, was the largest assortment of pots, pans, and utensils Marilee had ever seen. They were the tools of Jane's trade, along with the double ovens and enormous freezer which took up the space along an entire wall.

Jane offered her a warm scone and together they sipped tea and decided which meals for the cruise had to be cooked in advance and stored in the freezer. Next they made lists of cold meals, such as occasional breakfasts and lunches, that didn't require more than refrigerator or pantry space.

"We'll be stopping at several islands, so if I run out of fresh produce I can buy more on the way."

"Well, hurry up and get the supplies so I can spend the next two days cooking. While you're gone, I'll do the necessary baking. I have plenty of those ingredients." She paused, putting her hands on her hips. "This feels so good, just like when I prepared meals for your father's cruises."

Marilee grabbed the long list they'd made and headed for the door, wiping a tear away as she went.

*   *   *

The next morning, an early telephone call awakened Marilee. Mike had a possible buyer for the *Southern Star.*

"Really? That's fantastic. And about time. It seems like weeks since I asked you to try to sell her."

"That's not such a long time for something like this. Besides, things are slow just now. When the economy is down, yachts the size of yours aren't in great demand."

"When are they coming to look at her?" Marilee asked.

"This afternoon, about two, I believe. I can't come with them, but I know you can show the *Star* as well as I can. Maybe better."

"Great. That gives me plenty of time to have the *Star* looking shipshape for their inspection." She put down her cell phone and spent the next four hours shoving her belongings out of sight, cleaning the galley, and dusting furniture.

The Clarks, who showed up promptly at 2:00, looked too young to be retirees. They said they had retired early and were looking for an adventure while still agile enough to enjoy it. After an inspection that lasted an hour, they insisted they loved everything about the *Southern Star*—even the price—and said they were going back to the yacht broker's office to do the paperwork.

Marilee waited anxiously for a call from Mike, but at ten past four she could wait no longer and called him. "Tell me about those clients of yours. Have they signed an offer? How soon do they want possession?"

Mike sounded a little sheepish. "I'm sorry. I was just about to pick up the phone to call you. The Clarks changed their mind."

"Changed their mind?" The news almost knocked her down. She had to sit, her stomach muscles tightening in shock. "Why?" she managed in a strangled voice. "Did they say why?"

"No, not exactly. They were on their vacation and maybe got carried away thinking about retiring down here on a yacht. Then, well, I guess the reality of what that would mean must have hit them. I'm so sorry," he added again.

Marilee disconnected, feeling too upset to talk.

Gary took that very moment to arrive on board the *Star.* Feeling the need to tell somebody—to vent her frustration—she went out on deck and blurted out the awful story.

"Gee, that's too bad."

"I was sure they were going to buy it. More than sure: positive. And then suddenly they backed down. I still can't believe it."

Gary stood still for a moment, then said in a low tone, "I'm sorry."

"I had visions of not having to do this cruise for the Wellmans after all."

"Not doing the cruise? Why?"

"Because I wouldn't need money to make mortgage payments. The yacht would be sold."

Gary sat in one of the deck chairs. "That would be very optimistic of you, wouldn't it, thinking the deal would be closed and the proceeds in your hands within days?"

Marilee sat and ran a hand through her hair. "Yes, I guess you're right about that, but . . ."

"Besides," Gary added, "it wouldn't be very nice to cancel the Wellmans' cruise on such short notice. There's no time for them to book it with someone else."

"That's true, but I hadn't cashed the check they sent my dad yet. And you know I'm anxious to sell. My job pays pretty well, but no way can I afford to keep up a fifty-two-foot yacht."

"Not even the one your father owned and you sort of grew up on?" His voice had taken on a softer tone. "Don't you have memories—"

"I can't afford memories," she answered. Some of those memories were of Gary, and she wondered if he was deliberately trying to evoke them.

She forced herself to accept the reality and deal with it. So the sale fell through—she supposed things like that happened. She'd just have to get over it. One couple decided against buying the *Star,* but maybe the next one wouldn't.

She rose and changed the subject. "It's almost dinner time. If you came here hoping I'd fix something for you to eat, forget it. I'm going to Jane's. We'll snack in between wrapping dinners in foil for the freezer." She gave him a wicked smile. "Of course, you could join us— doing the wrapping, that is."

"Thanks, but no thanks. But I will stop by Jane's later and carry all those trays of meals back here for you."

"Don't pat yourself on the back for that small chore."

He gave her a mocking smile and headed toward the ship's railing.

"By the way," she asked, "why did you come here just now? I didn't expect you until tomorrow morning."

"Actually, I just wanted to see if you were ready for tomorrow. See if there was anything I could do to help. And, as you see, there was."

"I'll make a note," she said.

Marilee and Jane finished their work by nine that night, and then sat down wearily with cups of hot tea and some of Jane's homemade coffee cake.

"I can't believe we did all that tonight, but at least we don't have to truck it over to the *Star.* Gary promised to do that much for us."

"How are you and Gary getting along? Since he agreed to act as captain, I gather the unpleasant episode of eight years ago has been forgotten."

"Not forgotten. As I told you yesterday, he insisted on my coming along on the cruise—demanded it, in fact—or I wouldn't be here tonight. We have a sort of truce."

"That's not all bad. After all, if you crew for him, you won't have to pay someone else. This is a chance to make another payment to the bank while Mike tries to sell the *Star.*"

"That reminds me," Marilee said. "I thought for a little while that Mike had sold her. His buyers showed up at two and loved everything, and then they went back to Mike's office and immediately changed their minds."

"That's weird. I wonder if they were the couple I saw in his office this afternoon."

"You saw . . . wait a minute. What are you talking about? How did you see Mike? I thought you were cooking all day."

"I was. Well, almost all day. But I ran out of fresh ginger, and you know I like to buy certain spices and fruit at that little stand on the corner of Fourth. Mike's office is across the street, so I took him a ripe papaya. I know how he loves them."

Marilee felt her brow wrinkling. "Let me get this straight. You went into Mike's office with the papaya, and the couple was there saying they changed their minds."

"I don't know what they said before I got there, and they left when I came in."

"But Mike told you they said they changed their minds?"

"Not exactly. I really wasn't paying much attention, thinking I had to hurry back home. All I remember is him saying something about my providing the food for the cruise and how it wouldn't be fair to the Wellmans to cancel it."

Marilee put her teacup down so quickly it made a clinking sound on the saucer. "He *told* you it wouldn't be fair?"

"Oh, no, he wasn't talking to me then. He was talking to Gary."

Marilee's voice went up an octave. "Gary was there too?"

"Oh, yeah. Didn't I say that? Well, he was just leaving anyway." She gave Marilee a puzzled look. "Is there something I'm not getting? I know I can become a little confused when I'm as busy as I've been these past two days."

Marilee's throat almost closed and her breathing nearly stopped. "Mike and Gary were talking about the

Wellmans' cruise and Mike said it wouldn't be fair to cancel?"

Jane rubbed her chin. "Maybe Gary was the one who said that. I'm not sure."

"But Gary said the very same thing to me earlier tonight. Do you realize what that means?"

Jane shook her head.

"He screwed up the deal! Mike somehow talked the Clarks out of buying the *Star*!"

Jane frowned. "Oh, surely you're jumping to conclusions. Why would he do that?"

"I don't know, but he must have. I just can't believe the Clarks would change their minds so quickly. You should have heard them rave about the *Star*." She frowned and paced the floor.

Jane put out her arm. "Now don't go rushing to accuse him of something that might not be true. I saw him talking to Gary, but I really have no idea what was said beyond what I just told you."

Marilee had reached the opposite end of Jane's extralarge catering kitchen and turned to come striding back, just as she heard a knock on the front door. Jane went to answer it, and Gary came into the room.

"Well, here I am, ready to do my chores for you."

Marilee rushed up to him. "First, tell me what Mike said to you this afternoon."

The smile left his face. "We said a lot of things. What in particular do you want to know?"

"Jane overheard him tell you that the Clarks changed their mind about buying the *Star*. And I just don't believe that. He told them something that squashed the deal, and I want to know what."

"How should I know what he told them?"

Anger escalating, Marilee began pacing again. "I'll sue him! I'll tell the Yacht Brokers Association and have him sanctioned!"

In two long strides, Gary caught up with her and turned her about. "Calm down. You don't have any facts for such an accusation."

"Yes, I do. Jane overheard him tell you that it wasn't fair to cancel the Wellmans' cruise, and then you repeated that to me."

"That doesn't mean anything."

Marilee snatched her arm out of Gary's grip and headed for the telephone on Jane's wall. "I'm going to call Mike right now and tell him what I think of him."

Once more, Gary was behind her and took the receiver out of her hands. "You don't have to do that. I'll tell you the truth." He hung up the phone and steered Marilee to one of the wooden kitchen chairs. After a long pause, in which he rubbed his forehead as if trying to form the right words, he sat in one of the other chairs.

"Mike didn't put thumbs down on the deal. I did."

She didn't answer for a moment, hardly understanding what he said.

"When Mike was out of the office for a moment, I told the Clarks that you didn't really want to sell the *Star* and they left."

"But why would they believe you? Who did they think you were?"

Another long silence. "I told them I was your husband, and I didn't want you to sell her."

"You *what*!" For a brief moment, she wanted to throw herself on him and beat him with her fists, tear at his face with her nails. She did neither, but her expression should have turned him to stone.

"You told them you were my husband and broke up my deal to sell the *Star.* Why did you do that? Why . . . ?"

"Wait a minute—"

"No, I won't wait a minute, not a second. How could you be so mean and underhanded?"

Gary stood still in the center of the room, head down, as if he regretted his actions. She waited to see what excuse he would give, if any.

But no. When he raised his face to her, she saw no sign of remorse or sorrow. He'd been deep in thought, as if forming the right words to vindicate what he'd done.

"I didn't mean to have it turn out this way," he said finally. "It was supposed to be a joke. I just said I didn't think you wanted to sell the *Star* after all."

"But Mike told me the Clarks had changed their minds."

"Mike was just trying to let you down easy."

"No, he was trying to save you. He didn't want me to know you betrayed me."

Gary's expression changed at once. A smile appeared. "Hey, let's not get excited about this. Mike will find another buyer for you."

"But why did you do it?" She rose and stared at him until the answer came to her. "I know why. So I wouldn't cancel the cruise, and you wouldn't lose out on a skipper's fee."

"I'm not exactly desperate for money."

"To get back at me for refusing you eight years ago! I *knew* you wanted revenge. I should never have believed that friendly mask you put on, your eagerness to help me."

He stood. "I did want to help you. I do."

"So you sabotaged my sale. Is that what you call help?" She moved as far away from him as possible. "Well, I don't need any more of your help. Just get out of my sight!"

"I'll see you tomorrow morning."

"Omigod. The Wellmans. The cruise. I can't not do the cruise now, and I can't do it without you. You . . . you . . ." The right word—the truly offensive word to match her feelings toward him—refused to come.

He headed for the door. "You're taking this way too seriously, you know." He paused. "Look, I'm sorry, okay? But it will all work out, you'll see." He grasped the doorknob, then turned again. "How about this? I won't charge you a cent for the cruise."

Her body trembling with rage and frustration, Marilee picked up the plastic napkin holder from Jane's table and threw it at him. It hit the door with a loud crack and a dozen paper napkins exploded into the air, like flowers in a sudden wind.

Chapter Six

As the van carrying Gary and the four guests approached the marina, Marilee waited on the deck of the *Southern Star.* She smoothed the blouse she'd tucked into a cotton skirt—the outfit she had changed into after a mishap in the galley. Earlier that morning, she'd spilled a pot of coffee over herself, the remains of breakfast, and the floor.

It was just another in a long line of awful things that kept happening to her. First, her father dying and leaving the *Southern Star* to her with a mortgage she couldn't possibly handle. Then, despite what looked like good news, Gary agreeing to skipper the cruise so she could earn some money and insisting on her coming along as crew, no doubt to harass her. Finally, Mike finding a buyer for the yacht, and Gary souring the deal. Compared to all that, spilling the coffee, she had to admit, ranked low on the list. But that didn't mean she felt good about it.

Gary parked the van at the entrance to the boat

docks, and she watched his tall, rangy body with admiration. Effortlessly lifting out suitcases, he tucked one under each arm and held another in each hand. He walked toward the *Star,* accompanied by two men and two women who appeared to be in their early forties. He laughed and conversed as if he'd known them for years. They in turn seemed to be in good spirits, and it was obvious, even at a distance, that they were already enjoying Gary's company.

A sudden stab of annoyance returned. Had she not spilled the coffee it would have been she, and not Gary, who met the Wellman party at the airport. Instead, in the interest of time, Gary offered to make the trip and deposit the Wellmans' check at the bank while she changed clothes and cleaned the galley. It was not the most auspicious way to begin the cruise. She had planned to keep Gary in his place, introducing him as the temporary, hired skipper. Instead, unwittingly turning the tables, he would introduce her, elevating his position to one of authority. It was too infuriating, too frustrating, as everything else had been during the few days of preparations.

Everywhere she went Gary followed, seemingly bent on double-checking everything she did. Determined to get along, she refused to charge him with harassment. Nor was the situation helped by the looks he occasionally gave her, looks that indicated he thought her beautiful, looks which threatened to reinstate the longing she once had for him.

"Lee, here are your guests," he said, setting down the suitcases on the dock and lifting the rail so that the others could board the *Star.* "Marilee Shaw, the Wellmans."

"Welcome aboard." She smiled, then looked from one man to the other. "Which of you is Mr. Wellman?"

There was a slight pause, and then the shorter, heavier man laughed. "We both are." He stretched out his hand and gave hers a firm shake. "We're both Wellmans. We're brothers. And, please," he continued, "let's drop the last name formality. I'm Barry and this is my wife, Vicki."

He indicated the woman whose dark hair was short and whose dark gray pantsuit seemed totally out of place. After acknowledging her, Marilee turned to the other man.

"Tom Wellman," he said, introducing himself. He carried a rich brown leather attaché case and looked very much like a successful executive.

Marilee looked from one to the other, but could see no family resemblance. Tom was tall and thin, fair-haired, and had blue eyes. He was better-looking than his brother, who had darker, thinning hair, and less refined features.

He put his arm around a flashy blond woman, also dressed in a suit, although hers was a lighter color and had a fashionable-length skirt. "This is Kimberly."

It seemed obvious to Marilee that the Wellmans had money, judging not only by the expensive clothes, but by their jewelry. Kimberly's fingers sparkled with diamonds, and both women sported enough gold bracelets to fill a showcase.

Marilee had a moment's worry about the staterooms. She hoped they weren't expecting suites. But when they booked the cruise, they knew they weren't getting the *Queen Mary*.

"I'm happy to have you all aboard." She hoped *happy* would epitomize the cruise. She wasn't sure what she had expected, but the two couples lacked the casual looks of people about to start a ten-day adventure at sea. She stopped herself. So they were different. So what?

Gary finished putting their luggage on the deck and then disembarked again, calling over his shoulder. "Show everyone to their cabins, Lee, while I park the van."

She squelched the urge to feel upset at his ordering her about. Then she turned to the guests with a smile and asked them to follow her below, where she pointed out the ship's facilities. She held her breath when she opened the door to the smaller guest room, but Barry immediately volunteered to take it. Then she showed Tom and Kimberly into the larger one.

Tom looked about, seemingly pleased with the accommodations. He opened the few small storage cabinets.

"Do any of these lock?" he asked. He glanced down at the attaché case he still held.

Marilee's gaze circled the cabin. "I don't believe so. Will that be a problem?"

"Of course not," Kimberly said. Then she laughed. "My husband refuses to separate work from play. He drags that old case with him everywhere we go." She smiled at Tom. "I'm afraid you're becoming an incurable workaholic, darling."

"Now, Kimberly, you know I'm not that bad." A glint of humor showed in his eyes. "But if it will make you happy, I'll put the work aside and devote every waking minute of our vacation to you."

He winked at Marilee, and she smiled back at him. However long they had been married, and for all she knew they might be newlyweds, they seemed to share a camaraderie that allowed them to air their feelings without getting intense about it. That was how marriage ought to be. If she and Gary had married, would they have been as agreeable when their opinions differed?

Now what put that thought in her mind? She shook her head to clear it. She was going to get along with him, not renew their romance.

By the time Gary returned, she had explained all the routines to the Wellmans, and when he suggested they get under way, she agreed. Having practiced the procedure twice more since the day of their shake-down cruise, Marilee moved smoothly through her duties, then pointed out the location of the life vests to the guests. They assembled on the deck to watch the *Star* maneuver into open water.

The day was brilliant and the sea calm. Marilee went below to make sure everything was secure in the galley. She dried a few dishes and placed them in the cupboards behind the rails. Then she latched the cupboard doors so they wouldn't fall open in the unlikely event the vessel heeled.

When she returned to the deck, she found the others standing at the doorway of the wheelhouse. Gary was outlining the itinerary he had compiled, along with a brief history of the various islands they would visit— from Cat Island with its ancient stone forts, up past the sparsely settled and magnificently wild Exuma Cays, to

New Providence with its capital, Nassau. He spun tales of the Spanish Main, pirates, rumrunners and New England schooners, openly enjoying the role of tour guide, exhibiting a boundless knowledge of the area and the sea, and, in Marilee's view, basking quite shamelessly in everyone's admiration.

"We have scuba and snorkeling gear, as well as fishing poles, and of course there's plenty to see in Nassau."

"I'm looking forward to that," Vicki said.

"Is this a ship-to-shore radio?" Barry asked, stepping into the wheelhouse and fingering one of the dials set into the control panel. When Gary acknowledged that it was, he asked how far the band reached.

"We can pick up broadcasts from Miami," Gary said.

"That far?" Tom said. "Then we can get news from outside."

Marilee, remembering his conversation with his wife earlier, decided he hadn't meant his vow.

As everyone settled themselves into canvas deck chairs, Tom turned to Marilee. "I understand Gary knows Nassau well. On the drive from the airport he told us he lived there for almost six years."

She smiled, but didn't comment. She knew nothing about his activities during those years, and that reality made her face feel warm and her skin tight across her throat. Suddenly she wished she knew more about that time, then banished the thought as irrelevant.

Shortly after noon, she slipped down to the galley again, prepared iced tea and roast beef sandwiches, and served lunch. Afterward, she had time to sit topside and talk to the others, and before she knew it, the *Star* had reached Cape Eleuthera, near the southern tip of the island. Gary called to her to make ready to lower the anchor.

When all was secure and the engines shut down, she began preparations for dinner. She set out platters on a tray and was making canapes when Gary descended. Even before looking at him, she was aware he was staring at her. She felt the skin on the back of her neck prickle.

"Mmm," he said, helping himself to a thin square of toast heaped with a shredded crabmeat mixture. "This looks tempting."

As he popped the canape into his mouth, Marilee pushed the plate from his reach. "No more samples," she told him sternly. "These are for the paying guests."

He watched her in silence while she lay slices of hard-boiled egg onto crackers, topping each with a marinated artichoke heart. Then he said lightly, "Something's got the cook out of sorts this evening. It can't be the weather or the company. So far both have been excellent." He gave her a smile that sent a traitorous flutter into the pit of her stomach. Then his expression changed to one of mock seriousness. "And it can't be me."

She didn't answer.

He lounged against the counter, his long legs crossed in front of him. "What's the matter, Lee?"

"Nothing's the matter," she answered, making an effort at nonchalance. "It's a lovely trip. I'm having a marvelous time." She uncapped a jar of spicy French mustard and began to spoon it into a shallow bowl.

"No, you're not," he said in a casual tone, closing his

hand over hers. A tingling sensation skittered along her fingers, making her drop the spoon onto the counter. If he was at all aware of the effect of his touch on her, he gave no indication. "You're feeling put upon and you're looking for the handiest person to blame . . . which I suppose is me."

"That's not true." She disengaged her hand.

"But remember, Lee," he went on gently, "I worked all afternoon, driving to the airport and piloting the *Star* down here. You're not going to complain now that it's your turn to do a few chores?"

She snapped open the refrigerator and removed a package of cheese. "I'm not complaining," she said airily, "although I wouldn't define playing at social director all afternoon as Herculean labor." She smiled a Cheshire-cat smile at him and set the wedge of cheese and a knife onto a plate. "Everyone seems quite taken with your commentary, especially the ladies. It wouldn't surprise me if someone starts a Gary Pritchard fan club before the cruise is over."

He came up behind her and placed his hands on her shoulders. "Perhaps you'd like to spearhead the drive?"

"Absolutely not!" Her words were too heated and she relaxed before speaking again, difficult though it was with the touch of his hands and the familiar smell of his cologne disturbing her senses. "I was merely pointing out that your so-called work is hardly comparable to that of a stevedore, for example."

He nuzzled her ear, sending a delicious shiver down her back. Then he let his hands drop from her shoulders. "Be that as it may, we did assign certain tasks to certain persons, and this person is finished with his tasks for the day, and this person"—he tapped her gently on the tip of her nose—"is not."

She let the information sink in. Before she could comment, he said, "You know, Lee, when I crewed for your father during the summers when I was in college and the two years afterward, I served meals and washed dishes too. You, at least, know something about cooking. Jane had a real job teaching me how to fix her meals without incinerating everything. There isn't anything you have to do that I haven't done myself."

"I said I wasn't complaining, although you could get out of my way once in a while." She gave him a tight smile, and he stepped back against the refrigerator. In a moment, she turned again and signaled him to move once more. He left that position and this time lounged against the sink.

She removed ice from the freezer and placed it in a bucket, then turned to the sink, where he again blocked her movements. "Since you insist on being down here, you could make yourself useful," she commented. "Or have you forgotten all those little chores Jane taught you?"

"It would be my pleasure," he announced, and made a deep bow. "Ah, I have it!" He returned to the refrigerator and removed a jar of olives. He then opened and emptied them into a small bowl and, carrying it as if it were a scepter on a velvet cushion, ascended to the saloon.

Marilee felt her face warm and knew it was not because of the tropical air and the cramped quarters in the galley. She must get control of herself, not let him get under her skin that way. There were nine more days to go, and she could not allow his flippant attitude to make her miserable.

Plus, he was right. He was the captain and she had agreed to perform the other duties, so there was no point in being ungracious about it now.

Her tray ready at last, she ascended to the saloon and, seeing no one there, continued to the deck. Gary, having deposited the olives on the plank table, sat in a deck chair, legs crossed, discussing the islands with Barry and Tom Wellman. She set down the tray, suggested the men help themselves to whatever they wanted to drink, and returned to the galley where she picked up the platter of appetizers.

When she returned to the deck, the ladies had joined the men, wearing dresses Marilee thought more suitable for a Las Vegas nightclub. She hoped nothing got spilled on that silk. They would definitely not be making a pit stop for dry cleaning. Then she mentally rebuked herself. After all, the guests were new at yachting.

But she no sooner passed the platter of food and settled into a deck chair, when Gary said, "Lee, you've forgotten the Perrier. And we could use more ice too."

Teeth clenched, she returned to the galley. Her face furrowed into a frown, and she slammed her palm down on the counter. He was treating her like a servant while he, ensconced like a king, ordered her about.

She tried to compose herself before returning to the

deck, but couldn't get over her feelings. She pulled a tray from the freezer. "You want ice, Gary?" she muttered, plucking a cube from the tray. "I'll give you ice."

Concealing the cube of ice in one hand behind a full glass of water, she snatched a bottle of Perrier with the other and went on deck. As she placed the bottle of mineral water on the table, she smiled disarmingly. Then, walking toward Gary, she pretended to slip and fell forward, one arm reaching to grasp his where it rested on the chair. With the other, she tilted her glass dangerously close to him and dropped the ice cube down his shirt front.

She straightened again almost immediately, and Gary, apparently relieved to see that she hadn't spilled the glass of water over him, seemed unaware of what really happened.

"So sorry," she said. "I didn't spill it on you, did I?" She patted him solicitously, making sure the ice cube dropped still lower on his bare chest.

She smiled, her eyes focused on his face, delighted by the sudden reaction she saw there. His mouth opened as if he were about to say something. His eyes widened, and his body moved forward. Then, peering at her in wonder, he widened his mouth to a smile, relaxed, and settled back into the chair again.

"Nothing, really. Just a drop," and he glanced down at the wet spot beginning to form on his shirt.

So he was going to pretend nothing had happened, was he? Well, that was all right. She had evened the score and that was all that mattered. She continued her careful observation, however, grinning gleefully whenever he made occasional sudden grimaces and shifted in his chair.

After that, it was almost a pleasure to return to the galley. She actually smiled as she removed the chicken cordon bleu from the freezer and popped it into the oven. She could even bear Gary's playing gracious host at dinner, while she trudged back and forth with the food.

Later, after cleaning up in the galley, she returned to the saloon and joined the others in after-dinner coffee, enjoying the soft sounds of the evening and the sunset that spread swirls of orange and red throughout the night sky.

However, she was failing miserably in her attempts to ignore Gary's good looks and the old feelings he aroused in her. Feelings that threatened to grow into a repetition of those she'd had as a teenager. She couldn't, she wouldn't, fall in love with him again.

Chapter Seven

Before retiring for the night, Marilee took a brief stroll on deck. Staring into the darkening sky, she understood that her annoyance with Gary that day had been a reaction to him personally, not to anything he had done. His magnetism had drawn her in—as it always did—and she wanted to be the object of his attention, listen to his voice speaking only to her, feel his gaze sweep over her. Yes, she wanted that and it was not only foolish, but dangerous. Somehow she would have to resist his appeal, no matter what.

She had the added discomfort of a mild case of sunburn. Too late she realized she'd been exposed to the sun during the hottest part of the day and had failed to use sunblock. Her reddened skin voiced a protest that could not be denied. That, and the other events of the day, took their toll. After she applied salve onto her burning arms and shoulders, she slipped into her narrow bunk and fell almost instantly asleep.

Sometime during the night, however, she awakened

feeling suffocated. The breeze had died, making it warm and close in her quarters. She had raised the hatch several inches, but even that was not sufficient to move the stagnant air. Her discomfort escalating, she sought a cool spot on the sheet, but it was no use—the bunk was too narrow to provide an as-yet-unused section. Wherever she moved a leg or an arm, the heat from her body had already wilted the cotton.

Even her nightgown, which was fashioned from the sheerest summer fabric and reached only to her knees, felt unusually constricting. She lifted the hem and fanned herself in an effort to stir some life into the air, but it met with a decided lack of success. Finally, she decided she needed a few minutes on deck. Unwilling to appear in night clothes in public—in case the Wellmans chose a stroll on deck as well—she pulled off the nightgown and put on a pair of shorts and tank top.

She mounted the ladders to the deck in the bow, opposite from the one used by guests and for meals, and was enveloped by a night lit by a thousand, no, a million stars. Then a familiar laugh greeted her. Gary.

He wore faded cutoff jeans, very worn at the pockets. His chest, covered with a light matting of dark hair, was bare. The mere sight of him made her heart flutter.

"I see we both had the same idea. Those tiny cabins make sleeping difficult." He looked her over. "I'm glad to see you. Besides, I haven't had my revenge yet for the ice cube you introduced me to this evening."

She smiled again at the memory, walked to the rail, and lifted her face to the sea-scented air. Somewhere between leaving her cabin and gaining the deck, she had lost most of her irritation . . . along with her will to fight with Gary.

"Revenge? Do you always have your own way?"

"As I recall, I never had my way with you." His voice was hushed. His fingers came to rest on the rail, bringing his arms into a semicircle around her. In the quiet of the night, she heard the calm sea lick against the bow of the ship and the intake of his breath against her ear.

"Gary, don't."

"Don't what?" He brushed her cheek with his own. "Remind you? Or try to have my way with you?"

"Either one." Her voice quavered and she gripped the rail in front of her. The day's heat, trapped in the varnished wood, seeped through her splayed fingers like the heat that ignited in the pit of her stomach from his touch.

"Can you forget the past that easily? I thought I could"—he lifted a hand and touched her ear—"until the day you turned up on my doorstep."

"Stop."

The edge of his nail traced the curve of her cheek, her jaw, the smooth line of her throat. Her hand flew up to brush his fingers away but he captured it. He bent his head and trailed moist kisses along her fingertips, lingering with exquisite deliberation over each before his lips moved up her bare arm.

"You have beautiful skin." His mouth found the hollow at her elbow.

"Gary!" Why was she still there?

"Delicious skin," he added.

She felt his lips against her upper arm. She knew she should escape and go back to her cabin.

"It's very sunburned." The cold reproach she intended became lost in a throat that had gone suddenly dry.

With his other hand he swept her hair aside. "Very sunburned?" He kissed her ear. "Hardly. And certainly not everywhere." His fingers remained tangled in her hair, and then, exerting the slightest pressure, he forced her to turn toward him. His blue-eyed stare ranged over her face. "No, not everywhere."

She knew she must find the will to move away before the effect of what he was doing robbed her entirely of her wits.

Then his gaze locked on hers, and she felt her resolve slip. His eyes hypnotized her, and before she could galvanize body and mind into any form of action to stop him, his mouth was there, only a hair's breadth away.

"I see no sunburn here." His lips parted, brushed against hers lightly, almost playfully, and coaxed her into a brief, preliminary kiss that teased rather than tantalized.

She closed her eyes. This couldn't be happening. She wouldn't let it happen. But he kissed her again, in a sweeping kiss that plunged her down a dizzying spiral of delight. Restraint fled. Reason was abandoned. The hands that should have forced him to release her slipped behind his neck to become lost in the blue-black thatch of hair.

When his lips finally left hers, she gasped and pushed

him away forcefully. "You're not being fair." The words spilled out, a last line of flimsy defense from deep in her subconscious.

"Fair?" he said, moving close to her again, his breath warm against her cheek. "Maybe not. But I'm being honest." He traced the curve of her lower lip with his finger.

He kissed her again, a surprisingly sweet, light kiss. "I've always tried to be that. With myself and with you. That's why I'm giving you fair warning that we'll finish what we started eight years ago. You and I were always meant for each other, and you'll realize it before this cruise is over."

She stirred against him, barely hearing his words, until slowly, then with a jolt, she returned to reality. Her body stiffened and she backed away from him as far as the hands that now encircled her waist would allow.

"No." She shook her head.

"Yes." His eyes reflected the firmness of his decision.

Her hands closed into fists, and she pushed against his chest. "You're wrong. I—"

Swiftly, without warning, his arms closed around her and his mouth silenced what to him must have sounded like silly, ineffectual denials. Then he let her go just as quickly, leaving her shaken to her very core.

"Go to bed, Lee," he said gently, dropping his hands. "Although I'd like to go on kissing you, I won't."

The statement hardly reassured her. A slow fury built inside her and she spun away from him, wanting to shout her denial, but controlling the impulse for fear of waking the guests.

She spoke out firmly. "Whatever happened to the professionalism we were to exhibit on this cruise?"

He leaned against the sloping bulkhead of the vessel and jammed his hands into the pockets of his jeans.

"Professionalism? I never liked that word." He grinned, sending her blood pressure higher.

"Why not? It was your very own word."

"So it was." The teasing quality remained in his tone. "But now I've changed my mind."

She stared, furious at him for creating the situation and herself for allowing it to get out of control. Years before she had put her feelings for Gary into perfect perspective and in ten short minutes he had destroyed that illusion.

"Good night, Lee." He walked past her. "Get some sleep. You're going to have a busy day tomorrow."

Chapter Eight

Except for sailing into Current Cut, where water surged through the narrows at what seemed an alarming speed, cruising on the leeward side of Eleuthera was calm and gentle. Gary turned the *Star* south, keeping the rocks to starboard until well past the silted bars. Then it was east by south, aiming for Hatchet Bay sixteen miles away.

At breakfast, he had behaved casually, as if nothing had happened between them the night before, as if he hadn't issued a statement about their future together. Having awakened on the same uneasy note on which she had fallen back asleep, Marilee was determined to deliver a warning of her own. In the first light of dawn that morning, she had stormed the deck.

"Gary!" The single word carried with it all her pent-up frustration. "We need to talk right here and now. Before this cruise goes one knot farther—"

At that moment Barry Wellman appeared from the port side of the wheelhouse, and Marilee swallowed the rest of her speech. By the time breakfast was finished and the dishes washed and stowed away, her anger had turned inward. Gary, she admitted painfully, had not been the only one affected by the siren song of the sea and a night sky shot through with a million stars. To her everlasting consternation, she would carry a vivid picture of herself locked in his arms, her lips surrendering to his kiss.

Leaning against the rail, she watched Gary through the open cockpit door. He came out of the chair anchored behind the wheel and, with a sigh, stretched, flexing the muscles in his arms and back. An old yachting cap sat at a rakish angle atop his dark hair. Framed by the stark white walls of the bridge, his body, clad in tan T-shirt and jeans, looked fit and bronzed, his wide-legged stance suggesting more than a hint of self-assurance.

She pulled her gaze away and turned it toward the sea. They were passing near the Glass Window, a narrow isthmus where, from the vantage point of smooth water on the west, it was possible to see the Atlantic breaking on the rocky coast only a few hundred feet to windward. The sight usually excited her, except today, when Gary occupied her thoughts to the exclusion of almost everything else.

What had he been trying to prove the night before? That he could make her fall in love with him? Eight years before, when she was young and naive, she'd turned down his proposal for good reason. That day on the *Seafarer* he hadn't asked her if she loved him, although he declared his own feelings and asked her to marry him. Did he still love her? Or was he simply bent on waging a campaign to make up for her rejecting him years before?

She had no intention of surrendering to his demands. Okay, the way she reacted to his kisses proved her attraction to him. But love? No. The lessons of the past were clear. She wanted stability, a man she could count on fifty-two weeks a year. That wasn't Gary. She would not become a divorce statistic like her mother, nor open herself to heartache by becoming involved with the wrong man. But it would take all of her willpower to avoid an involvement with Gary.

"Lee, how about making some iced tea?"

At the sound of his voice, her thoughts scattered. She glanced up to find him settled back against the sea chair, his head turned to her, his gaze focused appreciatively on her face and hair.

Her earlier indignation surfaced. "Gary, I want to talk to you," she said. The Wellmans were somewhere below, well out of earshot, but after running into Barry that morning she knew she needed to be discreet. What she could not do was allow her dispute with Gary to turn into open warfare to the detriment of the cruise. The Wellmans—any client—deserved better than that.

She marched onto the bridge and stopped beside Gary's chair. He glanced at her, then his gaze returned to the horizon. Hers, quite against her better judgment, strayed to the muscles of his forearms, where the deep tan seemed brushed with the reddish-gold tones of the sun.

"Anytime, Lee. Shoot."

His words brought a momentary vision.

"Gary, about last night." She was in no mood for preambles. Best to get right to the point. "I don't think you quite appreciate—"

"Lee," he cut in, "there isn't anything about you I don't appreciate." He dropped one hand from the wheel and, before she knew it, had one of hers trapped in the well of his long fingers.

She tried to pull away. "Gary, this is serious."

He guided her forward until she was more in his line of sight. "How are we going to argue effectively if I can't see you?" His eyes, the upward tilt of his lips, displayed more than a hint of amusement. "That *is* what's on your mind, isn't it?"

"You're very perceptive in the daylight." She gave another wrench of her hand, only to meet with the same lack of success. "Is that a mood that overtakes you at sunrise?"

He laughed. "Is that what had you in such a temper this morning, my so-called lack of perception?" His frown was more mocking than serious.

"You know perfectly well what that was all about."

He raised an eyebrow. "Last night?"

"What else?" Marilee heard her voice slide into a higher octave, and warned herself to keep cool and not lose control.

He reeled her in toward him like a prize fish. "Now Lee, let's not hammer this thing into the ground. Last night, well, it just happened. We both knew it would, sooner or later. And we both wanted it. I'm not ashamed to admit that. Why should you be?"

She knew she should avoid this man. But how could she while at sea? "Let me go, you . . . you clod."

He brought her fingers to his mouth and barely managed to plant a kiss on the tips before she pulled her hand away.

"Don't you ever run out of epithets?" he asked dryly.

"Don't you ever recognize a simple request when it pops up and hits you in the face?" she countered. "Or must you persist in deliberately misunderstanding everything about the situation?"

She was breathing hard, careful to keep her distance once she was free of his grip, although the close confines of the bridge didn't allow generously for that. "If so," she continued, "then allow me to spell it out for you clearly and concisely. I do not want you to touch me ever again." She gave her head a shake for emphasis.

He let a beat go by. "Would it make you happy," he drawled easily, grinning, "if I wore a bell, like a cat, to warn you every time I came into your line of sight?"

She closed her eyes, clenched her fists, and counted silently to three. Why must he make it so impossibly hard for her to remain angry with him?

"You can't make me happy," she began again, composing herself. "That's the whole point."

His expression underwent a rapid change. The amusement was gone from his eyes, from around his lips.

"I don't want a casual affair," she added quickly. "Any more than I think you do. And since there is no possible future for us . . ."

He was silent a moment, digesting that. Then he said softly, "Personally, I'm not against an affair. It can be casual or mean something more. That's up to you. But

I'm not going to be a hypocrite and pretend that when I look at you I don't feel something very . . . basic."

She wasn't sure what he meant, but she was still hesitant about getting to the heart of the matter with him.

"But," he continued, "trust me. I'm also not in the habit of forcing myself on women. Long ago, Lee, we had something special. Or at least I thought we did. You thought so too, and if you'd stop running long enough, you'd admit it. What we once felt for each other normally leads to commitment. Last night I wanted to find out if a spark of that remained. For a moment, it seemed it did."

"All we ever had was my schoolgirl crush. I've grown up, Gary." That hadn't changed either, she realized. She was still denying her attraction. But she had no choice. He was as wrong for her then as he'd ever been.

His gaze scanned the horizon, and he kept the ship on course with the lightest touch of his hand on the wheel. The expression she saw flit across his face moments earlier had vanished. He looked very much in control again, comfortable even. He gave her another of his charming smiles. "Call it anything you like."

She shrugged. "Does it matter what label we use?"

"No, but eventually you'll think of something more, oh, puritanical and evasive."

"You're insulting," she said, although she wasn't really offended.

"And since you're twenty-six, I doubt I can be accused of robbing the cradle anymore."

Secretly, she was grateful he had gotten them back onto a lighter course. But they were getting nowhere, going at cross purposes. She imagined his endurance, for that was far greater than hers. Still, she couldn't resist a taunt.

"There are also some very uncomplimentary names for people who persist in unrealistic delusions."

"I'm sure you'll think of ten while you're getting the tea."

"Oh," she groaned. "You are so frustrating." She clasped her hands in front of her tightly, until the urge to do something violent passed. "We seem to have lost the entire point of this conversation," she said stiffly. "That's something else you're good at, twisting things around. You are devious, underhanded, shifty, sneaky, conniving—"

"Lee, come here."

"No." She didn't want to go to him, to have him touch her again and put another tiny chink in the barrier she had spent the night building.

"If I have to put this thing on automatic—"

"Gary! We're in a glass cage up here." A moment later she was standing beside the wheel.

"Would it make you feel better," he said, "to know that I understand perfectly the point you're trying to make? You do not want anything to do with me. Correct?"

"Yes." She stared at him. It couldn't be that simple.

His next words proved her entirely correct. "Okay, now let me make my point. We're meant for each other. You can deny that any which way you like now, but when the time comes, you'll know it's right. I won't push it. I'm willing to wait until you know you're ready. And willing. I wouldn't have it any other way." He kept his voice low, speaking slowly, as if choosing his words very carefully.

He paused, then flashed her a wide grin. "Now, mate, go on down to the galley and get me my ration of tea. Debating with you is turning out to be extremely thirsty work."

Chapter Nine

When she returned to the bridge with a tall, sweating glass of iced tea, Marilee found Gary all business.

"I thought we'd anchor off Hatchet Bay and spend time reef fishing." He handed her a chart with an arrow pointing to a cove. "The Wellmans ought to enjoy that."

Marilee, grateful his mood and conversation had altered, nodded. "Will we do any tuna or marlin fishing?"

"I wouldn't recommend it. These people are too inexperienced. It's hard work trying to land the big ones. Even the most serious fishermen, who know what they're doing, rarely bag a trophy-sized catch."

She folded the chart and put it aside. "Have you ever caught one?"

"No." He altered their course a notch to starboard. "I've pulled in a few that I threw back, but never anything worth displaying. The trouble with amateurs is you can't convince them their specimen is not only inedible but undersized. They want to bring everything they catch on board, hoping to drag it back, get their picture taken with it on the dock, and have it stuffed and mounted."

"A fisherman's dream," Marilee agreed. Then she laughed. "I remember going out with my dad once near Grand Bahama. I caught a beauty that must have weighed twenty pounds. Dad was going to have it mounted for me, but somehow there was a breakdown in communication at home and my mother cooked part of it for dinner."

"Poor Lee." Gary reached out and tousled her hair.

It was an innocent gesture, lasting mere seconds, but she shifted away from him and changed the subject.

"Speaking of our inexperienced guests, what's your opinion of them?"

"What do you mean?" he asked.

"Well, you've done lots of charters. Do they seem like the usual type of guests?"

"There are all types, even some who look like they hate the whole idea of fishing in the Bahamas."

"That's what I mean. I have the strangest feeling they didn't come on this cruise for the usual reasons. Barry is the only one whose skin looks like it gets an occasional dose of sun. The others would burn like bacon in a frying pan. And they all seem to be avoiding the sun anyway, the very thing that lures people to the islands. They haven't expressed much interest in fishing, either. I don't see Kimberly and Vicki getting bait on their Gucci pants."

After a moment, she added, "I can't figure them out.

Last night, for instance, I saw Tom and Kimberly go into the other couple's stateroom. They were in there a long time."

"That doesn't sound odd to me," Gary said. "They obviously wanted to talk."

"They're free to do that on deck, or in the saloon. Why sequester themselves in a tiny cabin?"

"Privacy. We all crave it once in a while."

Marilee remembered something else. "But have you noticed that none of them wears a wedding ring? And once when I called Vicki 'Mrs. Wellman,' she didn't answer."

"Lots of people live together without marriage today. And even if they don't feel committed to each other, a little hanky-panky is no doubt considered de rigueur for vacations. There's nothing suspicious about it."

He changed the subject. "Will you get the anchors ready? Hatchet Bay will be smooth enough for only one, but we'll need both for the reef."

Doing as instructed, she managed to put Gary out of her mind. But not the Wellmans. Once again they hadn't been on deck that day. Other guests spent all their time there, as if they couldn't get enough of the sights, sounds, and smells of the sea.

Then, as if denying her unspoken accusation, Barry Wellman suddenly appeared. "Can I do anything?"

"You can help with the stern anchor, if you like." She showed him how to release the winch, and they worked in silence for a few minutes. "Do you know anything about bone fishing?" she asked.

"Not really." In spite of his admitted ignorance, he

asked no questions about it, and Marilee was again puzzled at such uncharacteristic behavior. But just then the other three Wellmans appeared on deck. For the first time since the cruise began, the women wore shorts and sleeveless blouses. At last they were showing some interest. She also hoped they'd used plenty of sunscreen.

After shutting down the engines, Gary came up on deck with the fishing gear.

"I think we'll pass," Kimberly said, and she and Vicki ducked under the canvas awning.

"Don't be silly," Tom said. "Give it a chance."

"Darling, really . . ." she began, but Tom had already moved beside her. After a brief whispered conversation, the women acquiesced.

"The fish come into the shallows for feeding," Marilee explained, "so we'll row the dinghy to the reefs. Then you bait your hook and cast it gently. Or you can simply let the bait drift out to the fish. They're extremely skittish, so silence is essential."

"Did you hear that, Kimberly?" Tom laughed, but it sounded a little sarcastic.

Kimberly cuffed him on the arm. "Some men," she emphasized, "persist in clinging to that old stereotype of women. We can be quiet if necessary."

Barry frowned and said nothing, and Marilee went below for bait. She wondered if her father had had many customers who seemed so ill-suited to the adventure. Still, they were paying a lot of money for it, so she had to assume they were enjoying themselves in their own way.

While they fished, they separated from one another,

wading into the shallows with their rods. Marilee kept her distance from Gary, afraid of her seesawing emotions. He'd said he wouldn't force the issue with her, but it was probably wiser to keep some space between them. Yet, he moved with such strength and grace, was such an intensely physical man, that she found it difficult to keep her eyes from him.

Hours passed and, except for Marilee, everyone caught some of the three-to-five pound silver beauties. Ankle-deep in the emerald waters, she was reminded of her childhood reef-fishing with her father, and let her mind wander to those days.

Suddenly a fish took her bait. Startled, she pulled in too rapidly and it struck out for open water. Seconds later it had pulled a hundred feet of line off her reel. She lost her balance, staggered, and fell—landing knees down on the hard reef, splashing water in every direction, and scaring dozens more bonefish into bolting.

Gary sprang instantly to her side. "Are you okay?"

"Yes." While he pulled her upright and rescued her pole, she examined the bruises on her knees. Fortunately, they weren't serious. She had her fish, but there would be no more for a long time. "I'm afraid I've ruined the day for everyone else, though."

"It was time to go back, anyway." Gary released the fish from her line and let it swim out to sea. He put an arm around her waist and helped her across the slippery rocks to the dinghy. She could feel the warmth of his touch and it set her pulse pounding. She was relieved when they were finally back on board the *Star.*

Dinner that night was not as quiet as previously. The

Wellmans seemed jolly and joined the conversation about casting for bonefish.

"Some fisherman you turned out to be," Kimberly chided Tom. "I caught four of them, and you caught only one. From now on, I don't want to hear any more remarks about my not being good at sports."

"Sports?" Tom repeated. "All you did was stand in the water and let the fish come in and grab the bait!"

"If it was so easy, how come you didn't get more?"

"Because you women kept talking. Every time you hooked one, you made so much noise you chased all the other fish away."

"I don't know what you men are complaining about," Vicki said. "Barry caught more than enough, so our whispering once or twice couldn't have interfered that much. Did you get four, or five?" she asked him.

"Six, but who's counting?" He laughed loudly.

Marilee was relieved to see that they appeared to enjoy the experience. Maybe they were finally getting into the spirit of the cruise.

After dinner that night, Gary congratulated them all. Listening to him talk about the fine points of fishing, Marilee found herself wondering if he had always had such a way with people. He spoke neither too much nor too little, and although his knowledge of the islands was extensive, he never boasted. He drew everyone into the conversation, asking questions that were pertinent rather than inquisitive. Had he been that way eight years earlier, or had her perception of him been limited to her romantic daydreams?

And yet, in spite of his ability to be charming while

instructive, the enthusiasm the Wellmans had exhibited earlier began to wane. They didn't respond nearly as much as she would have expected. Sometimes they seemed not even to listen to Gary's comments, going off in their own little world, thinking of entirely different things.

Shaking off the mood, she reminded herself that their private thoughts were none of her business and left the group and took a short swim before retiring. Tired, she lay on her bunk, but was unable to fall asleep at once. Instead she listened for Gary, wondering if he would try to coax her on deck again. Or would he abide by his promise that morning not to pressure her into making a decision about him? In a strange way, she almost wished he'd try.

Chapter Ten

During the next three days, Gary seemed to do exactly as he promised. They left Eleuthera Island, skirted Exuma Sound, which could be as rough as open sea, and headed north toward the Atlantic and the reef along Cat Island. Because of its height, the island was visible long before they reached it, and as they drew closer, they could see the wrecked remains of ancient stone forts. Eventually they rounded Devil's Point and headed for Hawks Nest and the Bight, where they anchored and Marilee made a trip to the local store to purchase fresh tomatoes, milk, and bread.

They next sailed toward Great Exuma and anchored once again for fishing along the edge of the shelf, before it dropped off into deep water.

After Gary spent some time coaxing them into trying, Tom and Barry separated themselves from the others. Whether it was their belief they'd catch more fish that way or to have a private conversation, Marilee wasn't sure. But they were both successful in hooking almost a dozen fish, including wahoo, which Marilee prepared for dinner.

On the sixth day of the cruise, Gary proposed snorkeling along one of the many cays that skirted the western side of Exuma.

"That sounds interesting," Tom said. Marilee was happy to see that there were no objections from the women. The cruise they'd chartered was more than half over, and she wanted very much for them to feel they were getting their money's worth.

Gary rowed the dinghy to the edge of the reef, and Marilee distributed swim fins. Clinging to the side of the small boat, she demonstrated the way to wet the inside of the face mask, adjust it, and breathe through the tube. One by one, they slipped over the side into the water, practiced her instructions for a few moments, and then set off, facedown, toward the bay.

The water was breathtakingly clear, with every bit of coral and rock seeming near enough to touch. The colors were varied shades of green and blue, with here and there a brilliant touch of red or purple. Tiny fish darted by, their eyes bright, their backs striped in yellow and black or green with an occasional red slash. Watching the Wellmans move silently through the water, she felt considerably better about them. Had they not begun to show some enjoyment, she would have felt guilty taking their twenty-thousand-dollar check.

By the afternoon, everyone's confidence was high and Marilee no longer needed to cluck over the group like a mother hen. She allowed herself to drift some distance away from the dinghy and the others, whose snorkel tubes with their orange stripes at the top were visible bobbing on the water. She lowered her head and lazily kicked her feet, seeking a school of small fish she had sighted earlier.

Suddenly, she felt a touch on her leg. Swirling about, she found Gary behind her. She turned away again to swim toward the others, but his hand grasped her ankle and he pulled her back toward him. His head came within inches of hers, and through the window of the mask, his eyes looked gray instead of blue.

She felt herself unable to move away from his penetrating gaze, and he drew her down into the water with him.

Instinctively, as the sea closed over the top of her tube, she held her breath and kicked her fins rapidly in place, trying to remain afloat. He pulled her closer still to his body until their masks touched, and she felt his hands moving along her back, pressing her to him. She pushed at his shoulders, but he was too strong for her. As if in slow motion, she watched her hands slide off his smooth body and float at her sides. Then she felt him push her away gently. He put his hands under her elbows and boosted her up, so that she broke the surface of the water seconds later. When he bobbed up next to her, she pulled the mask from her face and stared angrily at him.

"Just what did you think you were doing?" she sputtered.

He removed the tube from his mouth. "I wasn't doing anything, Lee. Don't be a killjoy." He grinned.

She gave him a stony glare. "I'll thank you to limit

your exploring to the other creatures in the sea. The ones with real fins! And while you're at it, please try not to almost drown me again."

"You didn't almost drown and you know it. Come now, Lee, where's your humor? I got tired of looking at fish and found something that attracted me a lot more."

"Let's not go into that again." She wished she could match his playful mood and trade jibes with him, but being close to him had the effect of winding her up tighter than a watch spring.

"Gary—"

He studied her face. "I've been the perfect gentleman lately. Don't tell me you haven't noticed."

"I have," she said tartly, "but I don't trust you."

"Is that why you've been avoiding me?" He didn't wait for an answer. "It won't do you any good, you know. I made you a promise and I fully intend to keep it. One of these days you'll agree I was right."

"Gary, stay away from me. I don't want to be part of your life." She lowered her mask, drew the mouthpiece between her teeth, and pushed off, increasing the distance between them. Still, her legs felt weak as jellyfish and her arms trembled as they sliced the water. Why was he so confident they would make a commitment before the cruise was over? And what was she really afraid of, that she would fall in love with him again? Could he sense a weakening on her part, of which even she was unaware? Perhaps he was counting on the special magic of the islands to weave a spell over her.

She kicked the water furiously. "It was all over years ago, Gary Pritchard," she muttered, as if the words could give her the strength she needed to resist him. But in the core of her being, she began to realize it would take more than words to get her through the long, hot days and nights.

The next morning she found some beef jerky and raw potato and put them into a string bag, which she tied to her waist. She told the guests they could feed the fish while snorkeling, and, after a while, they agreed to try it. Gary rowed to another reef and explained how they could dive well below the surface by simply holding their breaths, and then blow out the tube to clear it after they surfaced. Tom and Barry agreed to try it, and Tom came up sputtering, momentarily having forgotten to stop breathing through the tube while he was below.

Gary pounded him on the back and Tom finally stopped coughing, assuring everyone he was perfectly all right. He tried to make a joke of it, but seemed uncomfortable. "I thought I was used to salt water, but that was a little too much."

"I think I'll pass that up," Vicki said. "I like floating on the top much better. It's so relaxing. I could do it forever."

"Yes," Kimberly admitted, "I never was much of a swimmer, but this is easy. I don't even need a life jacket—I feel as if I couldn't drown if I wanted to."

Gary had brought along his underwater camera, and when Marilee dove down to show Barry how to scrape the potato with his fingernail so that the fish could eat the pieces, a sudden flash of light told her he had taken their picture. She bobbed to the surface again, blowing air out of the tube, took another deep breath and

descended again, passing out bits of potato and beef
jerky to Barry. Soon they were surrounded by dozens of
hungry fish. But when Gary approached again with the
camera, Barry turned and swam in the opposite direction. Camera shy, Marilee figured. And she didn't really
blame him. He was easily twenty-five pounds overweight,
and the billowing swim trunks did little to slim him
down. With a shake of her head, she signaled to Gary
not to take any more pictures.

Then a large gray form came into view, and she recognized it as a grouper. Since none of the Wellmans were
nearby, she enjoyed watching it with Gary. It showed no
fear of them, and they stopped feeding the fish and just
studied the grouper as it swam closer, snapped up some
beef jerky that had fallen, and then disappeared out of
sight. Then she and Gary continued feeding the fish,
pointing out unusual specimens to each other. When
he aimed the camera at her, she didn't balk. Instead, she
struck a silly pose, and then went into a comic underwater ballet. Having a picture of her was about as close
to having her as he was going to get. She took the camera
from Gary, and he did a series of somersaults, conclud-
ing with a maneuver that left him looking like he was
standing on his head.

When the fish-feeding was over, she contented herself
with floating on the surface, occasionally kicking her
legs to move through the water to new areas, where she
could find different rock formations. It was so peaceful,
all she wanted was to give herself up to the beauty and
tranquility of the sea, where the spectrum of blues ran
from pale aqua to the deepest cobalt. She felt the hot

sun on her back, even through the film of water which covered her, and at that moment she knew she would have been content to stay in the islands forever.

Forever. But her father had died, and she was selling the *Star,* so she had no excuse ever to come again. She would never see Eleuthera. Never see Gary, or even think of him. Was that the forever she wanted?

Chapter Eleven

Marilee continued her exploration a while longer, then removed her mask and breathing tube. As she rolled over onto her back to float, she caught sight of the dinghy cutting toward her with Gary pulling on the oars. Soon he came alongside and slowed the small craft.

"Where are the others?" she asked him.

"They decided they'd had enough for now. After lunch I told Tom and Barry I'd take them over to Staniel Cay."

"Lunch!" Marilee threw her equipment over the side of the dinghy. "What time is it? Why didn't you call me?"

"Relax. I took care of it." Gary leaned over and reached for her. He took her firmly under the arms and lifted her out of the water.

"Oh." Marilee gave a little gasp, and he brought her over the side and deposited her on the floor of the dinghy between his wide-spread knees. The strong smell of salt, mingled with the coconut oil he sometimes used, clung to his skin. She moved into the bow of the boat.

"You gave them lunch?" Her throat was tight. "What did you make?"

"A salad. They wanted something light. But first I showed Tom and Barry how to use the radio." He shook his head. "I thought people went on cruises to forget about everything." He began to row away from the yacht.

Marilee looked up in alarm. "What are you doing? The *Star* is the other way."

He paused at the oars, resting them against his thighs.

"I'm kidnapping you."

"Gary, I don't have time to be kidnapped."

He began to grin, then his face broke into a wide smile. He laughed, and, realizing how silly she must have sounded, she laughed with him.

"Where are you taking me?"

"To a cave," he answered matter-of-factly, once more manning the oars. "It's very similar to the one they used in the film *Thunderball*. Did you see it?"

She let her fingers trail over the surface of the water. Now that her so-called kidnapping was an accomplished fact, she was beginning to enjoy it. "Yes, it's one of those James Bond movies. The late-night TV channels run them often, and I sometimes stay up to watch."

"Do you?" His look was admiring. "You surprise me, Lee. I never thought you enjoyed that sort of thing. You have such a sensible approach to life."

"Oh?" she said, mildly stung. "Then why am I allow- ing myself to be kidnapped and dragged off to an iso- lated cave by a handsome man who . . ." She literally bit her tongue as the last words slipped out.

That time it was Gary's turn to say, "Oh."

Marilee shrugged and, before he could make anything of it, immediately changed the subject. "Where is the cave?"

"Over there." He pointed. Following the direction of his hand, she could make out the entrance to a dark cave.

Shielding her eyes from the sun, she peered intently. Gradually, Gary rowed closer to the entrance.

"Can we go in?" she asked in a low tone.

"Of course. It's perfectly safe."

A few more sweeps of the oars and they were inside, the sun suddenly blotted out. For a few seconds it seemed pitch dark compared to the brightness outside, but gradually her eyes adjusted and she could make out the huge rocky walls of the cave. The light seemed blue within, the water murky, and the air smelled like a damp cellar, with fishy overtones.

"It's huge," she whispered.

"Why are you whispering?"

"I don't know, it just seems appropriate. I'm afraid my voice will echo, I guess."

"It's not illegal to be here, you know. You can shout if you like." With that he gave a yell, not unlike that of Tarzan. When he finished, he looked smug.

Marilee had put both hands to her ears, but she smiled. "Well, it seems we've both been hiding parts of our personality. I had no idea you could do that."

"You came to Eleuthera far too seldom during the years I was cruising the islands, playing juvenile delinquent."

"I don't remember you as juvenile at all," she said,

her voice very soft. "You always seemed a grown man to me."

"And you always seemed a beautiful woman to me."

She wanted to escape the mood he was apparently trying to evoke and laughed. "Even when I was thirteen years old? Come now, I was a brat and you know it!"

An enigmatic expression passed quickly over Gary's face, and then he abruptly changed the subject. "Let's explore." He aimed the dinghy toward the side of the cave, where he wound the bow line around an outcropping of sharp rocks. In a moment he had slipped over the side of the boat and was treading water.

"Is it deep?" she asked.

"Very, I believe. Come. We'll dive down and see."

Without a thought of it possibly being dangerous, she joined him. She folded her legs over the side of the dinghy and let go, sliding into the water next to him. She almost thought she could hear her own heart beat.

Without a word, Gary took her free hand and pulled her away from the safety of the boat. Together they swam toward the center of the cave, lazily, not making waves. Then, at a signal, they lowered their heads together and made a deep underwater dive.

The water was not as black as it had appeared on the surface. Marilee could make out shapes of fish swimming about, fish that were different from those she had seen in the shallower waters of the sunny reefs. Still holding hands, they moved through the marine life as if one with them—slowly, silently, in perfect accord. They surfaced for air simultaneously and descended again, and Marilee enjoyed the beauty of the cave and its creatures.

She wished she could stay below longer, or that she had an air tank.

After several dives in different places, they swam to the far side and clung to a large flat rock. They pulled up their feet so that they sat on a ledge, water lapping over their hips.

"That was beautiful," she said, her voice still low.

"I thought you'd enjoy it."

The ledge on which they sat was smooth, almost silky to the touch, and she wondered if anyone else had ever sat upon it before as they were doing. It was small, with barely enough room for both of them to sit side by side, their arms brushing one another. Again, she felt that same electricity charging the air around them and knew, without looking at his face, that he felt it too. Maybe that was why he had brought her to the cave. Certainly it created the perfect backdrop for romance.

She pushed herself off the ledge. "Gary, we'd better get back."

He slipped into the water beside her. "One more dive?"

"It's late. The Wellmans must be wondering where we've gone off to."

Gary's sigh echoed through the cave. "Lee, you don't have to hover over these people twenty-four hours a day. They could have come along if they'd wanted to." He pushed a wet shock of hair away from his face.

"You asked them to come with us?" His revelation was a total surprise.

"Of course. You don't think I'd just take off with you and leave them?" He gave her a look. "Or maybe you did."

"What does it matter?" She felt her cheeks flush. For once, she'd misjudged him.

He gave a low laugh. "What did you think, Lee, that I brought you here alone so I could seduce you?"

"You are incredibly insensitive, Gary." Her voice wavered and she turned her back on him, swimming toward the dinghy.

He caught her hand and pulled her back to him. "Would you like me to kiss you here, Lee?" He had her by the waist then, holding her possessively with strong hands. His voice was thick, his eyes hazy.

"No." She pushed against his chest.

"You're a liar, Lee," he breathed against her ear.

"And you're—"

He moved his head back and then his mouth claimed hers, his powerful legs treading water for both of them. For an instant she gave herself up to the moment, but then lashed out at him with both hands. He let her go with a laugh.

"Save your protests, Lee. They won't do you a bit of good."

"Save your threats, Gary Pritchard," she countered. "To catch this fish, you'll need better bait than that!"

Chapter Twelve

Nassau lay amid pristine white beaches and tall, elegant palms, sparkling like a precious jewel under a splash of golden sun. At least, that was how Marilee had always thought of it. She leaned against the starboard rail to catch a glimpse of Government House overlooking the town from high on a hill. She admired Prince George Wharf and the pink or red horse-drawn surreys that plied the streets of the city.

In the recent past, on those visits to her father, they had often taken the six-hour trip from Eleuthera for a long weekend. Never in the height of the season, however. He had been far too busy with clients. It was just as well. Coming at those odd times, they had been able to take their leisure in the shops and restaurants and at the major attractions without getting caught in a crush of tourists.

Gary eased the *Star* into a temporary berth at the yacht club, where the plan was for the Wellmans to spend two days and evenings sightseeing and dining on their own.

Gary had offered to make arrangements for a car and driver to be put at their disposal, and Marilee had combed through numerous travel brochures, circling in red ink the highlights she felt they'd most enjoy. Still, they seemed uninterested. Instead, they had spent several hours in the saloon late the evening before, leaning toward one another and talking in low tones, as if they were working out a totally different agenda than the one she had offered, one which they apparently felt no need to discuss with her or Gary.

Of course, it was entirely possible they had done their own research about Nassau and, not wishing to hurt her feelings, had decided to explore other attractions, perhaps stay overnight in more spacious quarters than the yacht provided. Or maybe they just wanted to shop till they dropped. Remembering the expensive clothes and jewelry the women wore—to say nothing of the Rolex watch Tom sported—it wouldn't surprise her in the least.

Marilee's own plans had been far less ambitious. She spent the first day aboard the *Star* stripping the beds and taking sheets, towels, and other items to a laundry, as well as shopping for fresh food while Gary went off on his own.

The second day, she allowed him to talk her into going to the beach with him. It was one, he promised, that she would find exceptionally breathtaking. Since the episode in the cave, he had neither said nor done anything of a suggestive nature. In fact, had he been anyone else, she might have thought him resigned to failure. And while she didn't fully trust him, she felt that a public beach would inhibit any ideas he might have to the contrary.

While Gary readied the ship for their day ashore, Marilee slipped out of her yellow shorts and blouse and into a bikini made of soft cotton with a subtle black and burgundy batik-like pattern running through it. The top tied in front at the midriff and it was accompanied by a matching skirt that had a similar waist closure.

She had seen it in a shop window in San Diego the previous summer while there on business, and had fallen in love with it. After she tried it on, not even what she considered an exorbitant price could keep her from buying it. Oddly enough, she'd never found an opportunity to wear it until now, but it was perfect. Since Gary was treating for lunch, she wanted something that would serve for beachwear and at the same time be decorous enough for most of the oceanside restaurants. Then she put on a pair of black canvas espadrilles that laced around her ankles.

She gave her hair a vigorous brushing until it shone with golden highlights. Constant exposure to the sun had lightened it considerably, and she swept it up and gave it several twists before fastening it securely with a large hair clip.

A light application of lipstick was followed with a dab of gloss on both lips. She considered adding the tiniest touch of mascara, but a reminder that swimming would only wash it away eventually, or worse, cause it to streak, ended that debate. Her long, thick lashes would have to stand on their own. Then she stuffed a towel, suntan lotion, and a small cosmetics case into a string bag and rushed onto the deck. She had less than five minutes to make her way down Bay Street to the harbor master's office, where she had promised to meet Gary.

In spite of the crowds, a not-unusual occurrence for that time of year, she picked him out immediately. Tall, broad, tan, all hard-toned muscle, she would never have mistaken him for a camera-toting, souvenir-hunting tourist. She felt a familiar rush of excitement glide through her. To her surprise, it was not followed by an immediate reminder that such feelings, where Gary Pritchard was concerned, were not only foolhardy, but dangerous. What did that mean? A change of heart? Before she had a chance to explore the matter further, she saw that Gary had spotted her in the crowd and was waving at her. She waved back and quickened her pace until she was almost running toward him.

"I'm late. Sorry," she said, mildly out of breath.

He stood back from her. "You look lovely, Lee." He grinned. "Did you go to all this trouble for me?"

"I didn't go to any trouble." She looked him straight in the eyes and even managed to sound a little annoyed at his accusation. "I'm not wearing anything different from what you've seen me in before." It took all her effort not to avert her gaze and give credence to his suspicions—suspicions, she belatedly and shamefully admitted to herself, that were all too true. The pains she had taken with her appearance were the result of an unconscious desire to please him. The admission disturbed her.

"Maybe it's the color," he said. "It looks wonderful on you." Then he took her by the hand and led her across the street. He stopped in front of a building where PARADISE

ISLAND YACHTS was stenciled in large block letters on the broad sweep of glass to the right of the door. Below, in smaller letters, was the legend MARINE ARCHITECTURE.

"I'll just be a moment." He pushed open the door to a small reception area, where a young woman sat at a desk. He spoke to her briefly, returning seconds later, dangling a set of keys from his hand. As it turned out, they belonged to a sleek white Jaguar, a two-seater of almost classic vintage but obviously kept in near-mint condition.

"It's beautiful," Marilee said, running the tip of a finger delicately over a gleaming fender. "Who's the lucky owner?"

Gary held the door while she slid into the passenger's seat, then walked around to the other side of the car. When he was beside her in the other smoke-gray leather bucket seat, he said, "It belongs to a friend of mine."

"He must be a very good friend to trust you with such a beautiful car." She scanned the magnificent wood-grained dash panel studded with gleaming chrome dials and knobs and gave a teasing laugh. "Are you sure you can handle it?"

He shifted into gear and eased down on the accelerator. "I should." He pulled away from the curb and into the flow of traffic. "I owned it for close to six years."

She turned toward him in surprise. "You owned it?" She couldn't ever remember Gary with a car. He never seemed to touch land long enough to need one.

"At one time it was my favorite toy."

"I can certainly believe that." Her gaze trailed over the sleek, sloping lines of the hood. "Why did you sell it?"

Gary didn't answer at first. Then he said, "It had served its purpose. The needs I had when I bought it changed considerably afterward."

"Oh." She nodded, as if she understood what those needs were, although she could have guessed. Simple arithmetic told her that he must have bought the car shortly after she had refused to marry him, when he left Eleuthera for other islands, dropping completely out of sight. Had he settled there in Nassau, running charters aboard *Seafarer*? He had spoken of needs. Had he managed to satisfy them in the almost-continual holiday atmosphere of the city?

She looked out the side window. The streets were filled with tourists milling about the hotel entrances and shops that lined Bay Street. A good many of them were female, young, attractive, and seemingly unattached. How many women over the years had sat beside Gary in this luxurious sports car, exactly where she was sitting then, thinking their own private thoughts, just as she was doing? They, too, would have found him very attractive. And intelligent. With the kind of rare humor that made you feel warm and alive. Quite plausibly, more than a few might even have fallen in love with him.

Gary cut into her thoughts. "We have a last stop to make, and then I promise to take you to my special beach."

With a jolt, Marilee realized they had come to a stop and were parked in a lot adjacent to one of the most expensive restaurants in Nassau. She had never been inside—the closest she had ever come was a glimpse through the window in front—but it was all polished brass, sleek wood, and crystal chandeliers. Not that she'd ever had a desire to dine there. The decor looked too studiously elegant, but she had heard the food was the best on the islands.

She looked down at her outfit and over to Gary, who was dressed as casually as she in a loose polo shirt over shorts.

"I've ordered a picnic," he said, as if attuned to her thoughts. "They do them very nicely here." He swung open the car door.

"A picnic? That sounds marvelous."

He was in and out of the restaurant in a matter of minutes. After stowing what appeared to be a very complicated picnic hamper—she counted at least six drawers and compartments of varying sizes—in the well behind the seats, he climbed in and they were off again.

A breeze tinged with a refreshing tang of salt she could almost taste rushed in through the open windows, cooling her skin where the hot sun slanted across her bare arm and midriff. Content, she settled back in her seat and leaned against the soft leather, gazing up through the windshield at a cornflower blue sky.

What she had expected to be a short drive to the beach turned into one of much longer duration. Although they chatted easily along the way, they seemed, to Marilee, a long time reaching their destination. Just when she was beginning to wonder if they were lost, Gary turned the car off the main road and onto what resembled little more than a wide path. He shifted to a lower gear and slowly maneuvered the car into a dense grove of palms surrounded by lush, verdant undergrowth.

"We're here," he announced, turning off the engine. He reached across her and pushed open the door, then slid out his side of the car.

She exited and looked around across the top of the car. "We're where? If there's a beach nearby, it's very cleverly concealed. I don't see any other cars or people." She'd expected an inundation of both, but then she'd also expected to be taken to one of the more populated areas closer to Nassau. This looked like the middle of nowhere.

"It's somewhat off the beaten path," Gary said, an understatement, as he hefted the picnic hamper and walked to the rear of the car. He opened the trunk and removed two large, multistriped terry beach towels, which he handed to her, and a large beach blanket.

"I drove in as close as I could. We'll have about a five-minute walk from here."

With her bag dangling from one hand and the towels clutched in the other, she followed him deeper into the grove. It was cool and dim, shaded by the umbrella-like fronds at the tops of the slender tree trunks. Wedges of sunlight sliced through the canopy, giving the whole scene a primeval look. In its quiet, unspoiled way, it reminded her of the underwater cave Gary had taken her to. As she had then, she felt awed, her respect for nature renewed.

The edge of the grove formed a lip that dropped sharply down onto a narrow beach, forming a semicircular bowl of fragile, pink-white sand. At best an eighth of a mile in length, it appeared to have been carved out of the forest. At the shoreline, an azure surf washed over scattered shells bleached white by the brilliant sun.

Gary slithered gracefully down the slope and set the hamper onto the beach. Then he turned back toward Marilee and held his arms up to her. Fitting his strong hands around her waist, he lifted her easily, swung her carefully over the ledge, and set her down lightly on the sand.

"Do you like my beach?" Walking a short distance away, he spread the blanket out, then took the towels from her and dropped them nearby.

"It's beautiful." Her gaze trailed over the pristine sand and clear, sparkling surf lapping gently at the shoreline. "Also, it's quite deserted," she accused him.

"Let's be grateful for that." He removed his canvas deck shoes and dropped them onto the sand. "I've had my fill of crowds. That's one of the reasons I eventually left Nassau and moved back to Eleuthera. The older I got, the more I cherished my privacy."

To Marilee, the last eight years of his life were a complete mystery, one she would very much have liked to solve. During those years she had thought of him often, frequently at first, then less and less as time passed. And never without feelings of guilt, or sometimes a desperate longing for things to have turned out differently.

But with the opportunity at hand for her to satisfy her curiosity, she felt awkward and hardly sure he wouldn't resent the intrusion. Also, it would take a certain degree of delicacy to pry into that part of his life without opening old wounds for both of them.

"Are you hungry yet?" Gary faced her from across

the blanket. "If not, I know the perfect way to stimulate the appetite." He eased out of his shirt and slacks, revealing blue swim trunks. "A little exercise," he said, moving to where she stood, her string bag tightly in front of her. "Mildly strenuous, but very stimulating. Are you game?"

The isolated setting made her more intensely aware of him than she had ever been before and, wondering exactly what he had in mind, her heart began to pound. His fingers closed around hers, and he pried the bag loose. His gaze never leaving her face, he tossed it aside. He looked as if he intended to sweep her into his arms. If he kissed her then, she feared she'd never be able to resist.

Chapter Thirteen

Marilee's voice was a whisper. "What exercise is that?"

"There's a reef about a hundred yards out. I'll race you to it. And, to show you how good a sport I am, I'll even give you a ten-stroke head start."

With a shuddering sigh, Marilee expelled the breath she'd been holding and shook her head to clear it.

"A race," she said. "Okay, you're on!"

She undid the laces around her ankles and stepped out of her shoes, then untied the skirt over her bikini. She didn't wait for him to announce the start, but ran through the hot sand to the water's edge and plunged in. Although she was certain he could beat her if he wanted to, he let her reach the reef first. She stood there for a while, gazing quietly at the beauty that surrounded them. How lucky she'd been to have spent her early years in this paradise and retain her link with it over the years. A strong sense of longing swept through her, and once again, she realized how much she missed these beautiful islands.

She felt on the verge of tears, and realizing that she was about to make a fool of herself in front of Gary, she took a deep breath and dove back into the water. He followed a moment later, and they swam back to shore.

She toweled off quickly, rubbing her skin hard. Gary stood a few feet away, watching her, and she wondered if he had guessed at the emotion that had touched her so deeply. It was something she didn't want to discuss with him. The course of her life was set. There was no room for sentiment.

She smiled. "That was a great idea. I'm hungry now."

He lifted the picnic hamper onto the corner of the blanket and dropped onto one knee, sliding open a long, shallow drawer than ran along the bottom of the hamper. It contained a white tablecloth, which he spread over the center of the blanket before adding linen napkins. Then he opened another compartment and lifted out a plate on which rested two of the largest lobsters she'd ever seen. The strategically cracked shells were a brilliant reddish-pink. She watched as he set out two forest-green china plates and two long, narrow forks to dig the meat out of the shells.

She gave a cry of excitement as he placed a lobster on each plate. "Gary, what a wonderful treat."

"I hope lobster is still your favorite seafood." Next, he pulled out a clear covered dish of heated drawn butter and piping hot biscuits.

"How did you ever remember?"

"Old memories die hard, I guess. At least for me." He looked up at her and she saw that he was smiling, that there was no evidence of bitterness in his tone or on his face.

"Now let's see what else is here." He opened the remaining compartments and held forth a corn souffle, deep-fried plantain slices, mango, papaya, and a pineapple.

"Something else I recall," he said. "You had the appetite of a football linebacker. Are you ready for this?"

"You didn't bring it all for me, I hope." She laughed, enjoying herself immensely even though he evoked memories that she thought had long ago been pushed aside. The lobster, which had been his favorite, had become hers too. They had eaten it often that last summer, broiled sometimes over a charcoal fire on a beach like this.

"Well, let's try to do this justice." He swept his hand toward the food-laden tablecloth. They sat opposite one another, and he handed her a plate with her lobster.

She forked a piece of meat from the claw and began to eat, then paused as he did the same. "Gary, would you consider it an invasion of your privacy if I asked you a personal question? You don't have to answer if you prefer not to," she added hurriedly.

He laughed under his breath. "You sound as if you want to ask a question, but you're not sure you want an answer."

"I do want an answer." She toyed with her fork, feeling awkward again, in spite of his good-natured acceptance of her prying. "You talked about moving to Nassau. Had you lived there these past years?"

"Since you and I broke up? Yes."

She could find no trace of regret in his tone, as if that part of his past no longer held any meaning for him.

"Except for two months on Cat Island," he added.

"Only two months?" She remembered the island as being quite lovely. "What made you leave so soon?"

"It was too quiet."

"I thought that was what you liked so much about Cat." She recalled the few times, that last summer they were together, that he'd taken her there.

His laugh was wry. "The last thing I needed then was solitude. In fact, what I needed was just the opposite."

"And Nassau . . . ?"

His look was open. ". . . was exactly the place for what I wanted: good times, with no commitments and no regrets."

"Oh." Marilee dropped her gaze to her plate. His meaning was more than clear.

"Lee?" He waited until she looked at him again.

"Don't turn away every time the subject comes up between us. What did you think I did after you left Eleuthera that summer? Cashed in all my worldly goods—such as they were—and locked myself away in some monastery?"

"I hadn't thought about it at all."

"Or about me?"

She met his gaze honestly. "I thought about you. And how you must have hated me."

"I never hated you," he said softly. "How could I? I loved you once.

"Anyway," he continued briskly, "it was an asset having a business that could be uprooted and started elsewhere. Most of my old clients caught up with me and there never seemed a dearth of new ones."

"You must have done very well," she commented, with a genuine sense of relief.

He nodded. "Better than I'd expected, to be honest. And then I came into a rather nice inheritance when my uncle Charles passed away almost five years ago."

"He did?" she asked. "I'm sorry to hear that." She recalled Gary having spoken of his uncle often, and always with great affection. It was that uncle with whom he had lived during his college years, after his parents had been killed in an automobile accident.

"I never thought he'd be that generous. He'd had no objections to my working in the Bahamas during summer vacations, but he never really approved of my moving there to make a living. In that respect he was like you, Lee. That kind of life was too quixotic, from his point of view."

His reference made her uneasy, but after that the conversation swung into a broad and comfortable range of subjects for the remainder of the meal, and, for her, the afternoon passed pleasantly. They had finished the food, including every bit of fruit.

Between the heat of the sun and eating so much at one sitting, she found it difficult to keep awake. With a mumbled apology, she stretched out, facedown, on her towel.

"Before you fall asleep," he said, "you need to protect yourself from the sun." He walked up the beach, picking up long pieces of driftwood, which he brought back and stuck in the sand next to her. Then he pulled the second beach towel from its place in the sand and draped it over the upturned driftwood, making a kind of lean-to that provided shade.

"There, we'll call it the 'Banana Cabana.' "

She laughed, curled up in its shade, and closed her eyes.

The sun was sloping closer to the horizon when she opened them again. Her first awareness was of the pungent scent of coconut oil. Her second, following almost immediately, was the delicious sensation of gently massaging fingers gliding over her back.

"Mmm," she murmured, "that feels good." She took a deep breath, drinking in the sweet, familiar fragrance of the oil. Then, as if the oil had suddenly acted as a catalyst, her mind cleared and everything became sharp and focused: the sea with its rolling surf, the desolate beach, and the man who had brought her here.

"Gary," she said, "I think that's enough."

He stopped and recapped the lotion. "Sure."

A tiny tremor started deep inside her and spread swiftly through her limbs. Why had she come to this deserted beach with him anyway? What had she thought it would lead to, or had she bothered to think that far? She felt drawn by a force she couldn't control, and yet, facing the realization of the inevitability of this moment, she needed time to sort out her conflicting emotions.

"Gary . . . I . . ." She didn't finish. She turned onto her back but didn't rise, unable to explain the ambivalence of her feelings, hardly understanding them herself. All she knew was that she felt torn between her sudden wish to relive the past and her deeply imbedded fear of making a serious commitment to him.

Suddenly he leaned over and kissed her. For a long moment she responded to his kiss, wishing him never to stop. Then reality intruded once more. She pushed him aside, got to her knees, then stood unsteadily in the hot sand. She turned away from him, ran toward the sea and skirted the shoreline, feeling the gritty texture of the sand beneath her feet. He made no move to come after her and she stopped, letting the pale, frothy water swirl around her ankles, with the only sound the gentle slap of the waves.

He had said he wouldn't pressure her and, except for that brief kiss, he was keeping his promise. Why, then, did it bother her? She turned her gaze back to where he sat watching her. She realized she wanted more than a day of fun in the sun. She too wanted what they'd had before. But it was too late. They were older and she, at least, a bit wiser. Life could not be ad-libbed. You made sensible choices or you paid for them later in pain and heartbreak.

She retraced her path back to the beach blanket and fastened her skirt around her waist. "It's time to get back." Her words were the faintest whisper.

He pulled on his shorts and shirt as if he desired nothing more than to please her every whim. "It's too early to go back to the *Star*. How about sightseeing in Nassau?"

"That sounds fine," she said. And a lot safer than staying on a romantic beach with a man she used to love.

Chapter Fourteen

Marilee and Gary joined the throngs on Nassau's crowded streets. Weaving their way through happy vacationers, and playing tourist as well, they stopped for tea at a sidewalk café. Gary reached into his tote and retrieved the snapshots he had taken so far on the cruise.

They took turns scanning the prints and laughing at some of the funny faces Marilee had deliberately made when she thought Gary took too many of her. He had shots of the grouper who had startled them all and of the Wellmans feeding the smaller fish.

Once more, she noted that none of the Wellmans had let their faces be filmed.

"Don't you think it's odd? You've done dozens of charters. Don't most guests want their picture taken?"

"Most, yes, but not all." He paused. "Still, I agree with you that this particular batch is unquestionably camera-shy. And considering their masks covered most of their faces, they could hardly be recognized, anyway."

"I wonder what they're doing here in Nassau. They

took off in a hurry yesterday morning, and I thought they took a lot of their things with them, more than they'd need for two days, I would think."

"Well, you know those two women. They liked to have a different outfit for every occasion."

"I suppose you're right. I've never been that wealthy myself. I guess I don't know how the other half lives."

They strolled along the public beach. At dinnertime Gary chose a sidewalk restaurant. Then he took her to a nightclub in an area frequented by locals. They sat under the partial roof that edged a wooden platform, lit by the fires of a dozen torches, and watched the limbo dancers gyrate their shiny dark bodies to the lively beat of the music.

"How on earth can they do that?" she asked.

"Practice," he answered. "Want to try?" He grasped her hand, as if he would pull her onto the platform so she could take a turn at limbo dancing.

"Not on your life!"

Time after time, the dancers snaked their way beneath the poles, only to see them lowered still further for the next time. The steel drum band increased its tempo, and finally the performance ended in a noisy crescendo. She applauded wildly and caught Gary looking at her with a strange smile on his face.

"What's the matter?"

"Nothing. You look, well, as enthusiastic as ever. I love your zest for life." He leaned toward her and, without making a move to embrace her, placed his lips on hers in a soft, lingering kiss.

She held still, not breathing, feeling his mouth on

hers. It was as sweet as that kiss at the beach earlier. When he broke from her at last, she still didn't move, and her eyes were closed. Then she felt him rise from the seat next to her and her eyes snapped open.

"Time to go," he said. "I'd better get you back on board the *Star* before we turn into pumpkins."

She laughed with him and they left, arm in arm, like good chums who enjoyed being together regularly, who kissed only in friendship. Not like lovers. So why did that bother her?

The last remnants of sleep disappeared with the sun slanting into the porthole over her bunk. In a moment the events of the previous day and night rushed in, and a warmth swept over her body. She stretched lazily and her mouth turned up in a satisfied smile, her mind replaying in vivid detail every moment of the day she had shared with Gary.

They had become close during the hours on the beach. She felt she knew him better than she ever had before. And, although the setting was ideal for them to have shared more than a picnic lunch, Gary made no attempts to do more than kiss her, nor made any comments about her attitude. He spent the rest of the day acting the perfect escort, making her laugh, making her feel like a teenager again.

She turned toward the wall separating their two tiny cabins, wondering if Gary was still in his bed. If not, he hadn't awakened her, and, sitting up and drawing her knees tight against her body, she realized that she very much wished he had. Her constant awareness of him brought a flush to her cheeks. With a sigh, she knocked on the thin wall.

"Gary," she called, but there was no answer. Then she smelled the unmistakable aroma of brewing coffee.

She jumped up and dashed into the shower. The cool water tingled on her skin, causing a sharp intake of breath, but in moments the first shock had turned to exhilaration. Why did she suddenly feel so alive? She plunged her head under the running water. It was just what she needed, a cold shower! Then she shampooed her hair vigorously, using up some of her pent-up energy. Finally toweled dry, her hair damp and beginning to wave on her neck, she returned to her quarters and slipped into her pink shorts and tank top.

Gary was in the galley fixing breakfast when she made her way up the ladder.

She took the apron from around his waist. "That's my job."

He planted a light kiss on the top of her head, and she had a sudden urge to kiss him back but resisted. Perhaps she shouldn't spoil the easy camaraderie they had achieved.

"See you," he said, and, taking the ladder two steps at a time, disappeared into the saloon.

She could hear voices coming from the deck and decided that the Wellmans must be there already. She poured a glass of orange juice and took a sip, then turned her attention to breakfast.

For once, doing the chores didn't spawn any feelings of resentment. She had only kind thoughts for everyone that morning. How lovely the galley was, how shiny and efficient. She came close to burning her hand on the stove top, where she had somehow left a burner on, but, with only the slightest shrug, continued smiling, remembering her day with Gary. She had never been so happy.

When they returned to the *Star* the night before, no lights showed in the saloon, so they assumed the Wellmans were already asleep. Removing her shoes, she crept silently along the deck. Before she slipped into her room, Gary had put his hands on her cheeks, looked deeply into her eyes, and kissed her gently on the mouth, saying, "Good night, Lee."

She had smiled up at him, wanting to let him know she understood what he meant, but could think of nothing to say. Words were unnecessary. They had achieved a rapport without them.

Now, heavy tray in hand, she made her way up the ladder to the saloon, then to the deck. Exhilarated, she turned her face up to the sky. Had it ever looked so blue? Or the water so crystal clear? Unable to keep from smiling, she strolled to the table, ready to set breakfast down in front of the Wellmans. What lovely people they were, what a marvelous cruise.

But they weren't there. Instead, Gary stood at the rail talking to two men on the dock, two men who looked suspiciously like policemen of some sort.

She almost felt the bubble of her happiness burst inside. A little knot of pain started in her midriff, and, seeing the frown on Gary's face, she felt it spread. Something was terribly wrong. With shaking knees she set down the tray, but before she could join them, the men walked off and Gary turned to her, his face a tight mask.

"What happened?" she asked, almost afraid to hear. "Where are the Wellmans? Are they awake? What's wrong?" The joy she felt earlier dissolved like snow in July.

He took her hand and led her to a deck chair, sat down facing her, and spoke quietly, almost as one would to a child. "I'm afraid I have bad news. The Wellmans weren't in their cabins last night. They skipped out."

"Skipped out? I don't understand. Skipped out where?"

"I've just been talking to the Nassau police. Their names aren't Wellman at all and they're wanted for forgery, embezzlement, and a few other things."

She couldn't speak. A hundred questions crowded her brain, while an unseen hammer beat a tattoo on her temples. Now all those little uncertainties she'd had about their guests began to make sense. "But their clothes and other things are still below, aren't they?"

"I suspect we'll find only empty suitcases. They each had two large ones, you know. They could have crammed what they needed into one and just left the others behind."

"To throw us off the track?"

"In case we looked in their cabin. They took off by plane right after we docked yesterday, so they have a good head start, but the authorities are trying to trace them." He paused. "I'm sorry, but it looks pretty bad."

The events of the past few days shifted into place in her head. "I don't understand. Okay, so their name isn't Wellman and they left Nassau for parts unknown. But what does that have to do with me? What's bad about that, except we'll go back to Eleuthera alone?"

He didn't answer, but suddenly she didn't need him to. The answer came to her plainly, horribly. The payment they'd made for the cruise was no payment at all!

"I suspect the check they gave you won't clear the bank," Gary said.

That lovely twenty thousand dollars that would make two payments on the *Star,* that would pay Gary for acting as skipper and Jane for the catering, that had already bought fuel and food—with her own checks that would bounce like rubber balls!—no longer existed. She sagged, and thought for a moment she would fall right out of the chair.

A wave of dizziness swept over her and perspiration slid down her neck, making her hair cling to her scalp.

Gary came to her, offering her a cup of the coffee she had brought up from the galley only moments before. "Here, drink this," he said, forcing the mug to her lips.

She gulped at it obediently, and let the hot bitter liquid burn her tongue and slide down her throat until she choked because she couldn't swallow. Tears of pain and frustration filled her eyes. Gary's arms went around her and she pressed her face into his broad chest; she let sobs rack her body. Why had this happened? Why, of all times, now?

An hour later they headed back to Eleuthera Island. Standing at the bow, Marilee turned her face up to the sky. Why, when her world had just fallen apart, did the weather have to be so perfect, mocking her? Never again would she stand there like this and feel the soft breeze in her face. The bank would foreclose on the *Star* and it would be sold for the balance of the mortgage.

True, she had intended to sell it anyway. It was only a sad reminder of her father, and of falling in love with Gary, to say nothing of the fact she could hardly own a yacht in Nassau when her job was in California. But to have it go like this was a worse fate than she deserved.

Her final sail on the yacht was over. Where had the ten days gone? Surely it was only yesterday that they had started out and Gary had promised to make her admit she still loved him. Now they were on their way back and, whether he realized it or not, he had come very close to making good on that promise.

A frown puckered her forehead, and a sudden uneasiness took hold in the pit of her stomach. What about Gary? She left the bow, where she had been standing at the rail, and strode back toward the bridge. As she drew near, Gary smiled at her, but she merely continued to walk the deck, deep in thought.

She knew that the past was not dead after all, never had been really. She would have to go back to California knowing that part of her would always remain here, with him. And what about her inescapable reasons for why it should end that way again? He was still the same Gary Pritchard, living a nomad's existence at sea, and she was still a woman who wanted a stable life and a husband who came home to her each evening. Did the past week change anything for either of them?

Gary didn't leave the bridge for lunch, saying he preferred to have a sandwich and some iced tea where he was. Afterward she went to him, hoping he would say something to place the situation into its proper perspective.

"Gary?"

"Yes?" He glanced away from the horizon only briefly.

"Can we talk?"

"Of course. I don't know what good it will do, though. I'm afraid I don't know what you can do about the Wellmans or the bad check."

"Not that."

"What then?"

Marilee was stung. She had frequently accused him of being insensitive, although on numerous occasions during the cruise he had proved otherwise, but surely he must be aware of the nature of her thoughts now. What about the vow he'd made to her? Or the moments they had shared yesterday? Had he forgotten already how close they had become the day before? Had it been only a casual encounter for him? In that event, perhaps it wouldn't occur to him that it might mean more to her. But what *did* it mean to her?

Biting her lower lip, she leaned back against the bulkhead. If she couldn't understand her own reaction to their new relationship, how could she discuss it with him?

Silence lengthened between them. Gary's eyes seemed veiled, as if he were not even watching their course, but thinking private thoughts he couldn't—or wouldn't—share.

"Nothing," she said, finally breaking the quiet. It was

too difficult for her to broach the subject, and she left the bridge to go below. She threw herself on the bunk and stared up at the ceiling, trying to put her thoughts in order and make some sense of them.

She must have dozed. The next thing she knew, Gary was calling loudly, "Lee, I need you," and she rushed topside again to find he had sighted Eleuthera, and she was needed to ready the anchors and lines.

Finally she heaved the stern line onto the dock, ran forward and did the same for the bow line, and then leaped expertly off the deck of the *Star* onto the wooden planks, fastening the lines with practiced hands.

"There you are!"

At the sound of the masculine voice at her ear, Marilee whipped her head around. She had thought she'd had about as many surprises as she could stand during the past ten days, but it appeared fate had just one more in store for her. Approaching her, looking incongruous in his tailored dark blue suit, white shirt, and silk tie, was Howard.

Chapter Fifteen

Marilee's throat tightened. Like a plant that had taken instant root, she simply stood and watched him come closer. He set down a camel-colored suitcase and matching attaché case and pulled off his jacket, leaving it on top. Then he rushed forward, planted his hands on her shoulders, and kissed her fervently. The combination of his quick movement and her surprise caused her to lose her balance momentarily, and, afraid she might fall backward into the water at the edge of the dock, she reached out and grabbed him.

"Howard!" she said when her mouth was free. "Why aren't you in California?"

"I came to see what had happened to you." His arms tightened around her. "You can't imagine how worried I've been. Also, I missed you, Marilee."

"But you knew—" She was at a loss for words. In the back of her mind was the certainty that dozens of people might be watching this little scene and drawing conclusions. She pulled away from his embrace.

"I have to secure the ship." She ran to the bow line that lay loose on the dock. As she wrapped and knotted it tightly, she glanced up to the bridge, but Gary was nowhere in sight.

Howard rushed up again. "You've been gone so long."

"The company gave me two months to settle Dad's affairs. It's not up yet." Why was she becoming so defensive and angry with Howard? She took a deep breath and tried to compose herself.

"You didn't call or write or answer my e-mails. Naturally, I worried. I had to telephone all over the island before I found someone to tell me you weren't even here, but out on a cruise. I didn't know what to think. I decided to find out for myself."

"It's a long story, Howard." She walked back quickly to the opening at the side of the ship's railing, where she put down the small gangplank.

As she worked he hovered over her, getting in her way, speaking earnestly and constantly. "Why on earth did you go off on a cruise?" Then he suddenly seemed to realize they were in a public place. "Can we go somewhere and talk? I'm booked at the Royal."

"Later. Please let me just finish this."

Instead, Howard pressed closer to her. "Why did you go sailing? You told me you were just going to sell the boat."

"Yacht," she corrected automatically. "My father had left a cruise on the books. People were expecting to go."

"People? What people? You didn't tell me you were going to be with other people down here."

"They—the Wellmans I mean—they were clients. At least I thought they were. I'll tell you all about it later." How could she possibly explain what had happened to them? The very thought of it would make her want to cry again, or scream. But Howard wasn't listening anyway.

"And who's that?"

His change of tone was unmistakable. He had seen Gary.

Marilee looked up and saw the tall bronzed figure making fast the dinghy in its accustomed berth on the roof. When he turned his gaze on her and the man next to her, her heart seemed to leap into her throat.

She turned back to Howard. "There are things I have to do," she said evasively. "Why don't I meet you later?"

"I don't see why we can't talk right now."

"Please try to understand. Why don't you check into the hotel, and I'll be there in an hour. I promise."

The tightness around Howard's lips told her he was not satisfied with her answer. He brushed his straight, sandy-colored hair back from his high forehead with one hand, then picked up his suitcases and jacket. "In an hour, then."

She watched him walk away, and then turned around.

Gary appeared at the stern of the yacht. "So that's Howard, the accountant."

His tone was light, bantering, yet different somehow. He sounded like the Gary she had spoken to at his house the day she asked him to captain the *Star,* not the Gary of the last two days. It was as if the cruise had never happened.

"Lawyer," she corrected.

"Oh, yes, Mr. Reliable."

"Gary—"

"The man you've been trying to fall in love with."

"Will you please—?"

But he didn't let her continue. "Your friendship seems to have progressed to the kissing stage at least." He gave her a maddening smile.

Why did he have to see that? She found herself thinking of excuses to make for it, then stopped. Gary, she reminded herself, had said nothing about his own feelings for her. In fact, if the smile he'd given her was any indication, he seemed amused rather than upset by the scene he'd witnessed.

"Whether you're in love with this Howard or not, Lee, he's definitely in love with you."

"What?"

"It's written on his face in neon letters."

And why should you care, she wanted to shout at him. But she bit back the words. Maybe this was a joke to him. For her, it was an extremely serious matter. Of course Howard cared—he was not a man to waste time and money on a woman for no purpose—but how could Gary tell from his brief glimpse? She watched his face, looking for some sign that he was jealous or that he cared at all. Whatever thoughts were going through his mind, he wasn't about to share them.

"Gary, I have to go." She felt hurt by his attitude, wanting more from him than amused laughter and jokes that were not especially funny.

"I'm leaving now, myself," he said. "I think everything is back in order on the bridge. If there's any problem, or if the police need to ask me any further questions about the Wellmans, you know where to find me." With a last, close look into her face, but still smiling wryly, he turned and stepped over the railing onto the dock. "And, Lee, I want you to know that under the circumstances, you don't have to pay me anything. Let's just say it was a favor done by one friend for another. After all, what are friends for?"

She watched him walk away, his last remark driving into her middle like a burning poker. How dare he? Why would he say such a thing? They had been so close these past few days. Just that morning he had kissed her again, smiling as if she was the most important person in his life. But then he was able to leave her with a remark about being *friends?*

An hour later, feeling both tense and awkward, she entered the lobby of the Eleuthera Royal Hotel, dressed in a freshly pressed fuschia-print sundress.

One of the few hotels in the area, the Royal was somewhat of a euphemism for its simple, almost rustic decor. She glanced around at the bamboo furniture and profusion of green plants in clay pots. Howard popped up from a chair behind one of them. He, too, had changed and was wearing more comfortable-looking clothes—tan knit trousers and a brown short-sleeved shirt.

"Marilee!" Again, he embraced her. Embarrassed by his twice showing emotion in a public place—not at all Howard's style—she pulled away quickly and led him toward the entrance of the little café off the lobby.

"I'd love a cup of tea," she said, hoping she didn't look as miserable as she felt.

Seated at a glass-topped table in a corner—she had chosen a table behind another of the inevitable potted palms—she twisted her hands nervously in her lap until the tea was finally served. Howard, meanwhile, kept up a constant stream of idle chatter—she guessed he was as nervous as she—about his law practice, the current awful state of politics in California, the unseasonable weather, and what he'd been doing in her absence.

"I feel like months have passed since you left, instead of only six-odd weeks," he said earnestly, looking intently into her eyes. "Have you accomplished everything yet?"

She told the whole long story—related her distress at finding that her father's bills exceeded his bank balance, how she had decided to conduct the final cruise on his books in order to make the additional mortgage payments, and how the Wellmans had turned out to be embezzlers, leaving her with more bills than before and ten days less time to do anything about them.

Finally she mentioned Gary, but didn't reveal the entire truth, referring to him only as a hired skipper who had worked for her father many years before.

Howard was not to be put off on that score, however. "He's the tall fellow with the cap and the"—he swallowed before he continued—"the rather proprietary look in his eyes when he saw you with me."

Marilee's palms were moist again and her breathing strained. "Don't be silly."

"Not that I blame him, Marilee," Howard rushed on, placing his hand over hers in what very much resembled a possessive signal of his own. That, along with the turn in conversation, made her more than a little uneasy.

"Your imagination is playing tricks on you," she said. She wished they could go back to talking about the weather, or anything else. Even politics couldn't be as volatile a subject as Gary Pritchard.

"If you want the truth, I'm more than a little jealous myself." He continued to stare at her with an earnest look, and finally she dropped her own gaze and smoothed her skirt in a mindless gesture, wishing for the tenth time that Howard had not chosen that particular moment to appear. That he had come at all was unfortunate enough, after the past ten days. With a determined effort, she pushed all thoughts of Gary and her financial condition away and tried to concentrate on Howard's words.

"We've known each other for almost a year. I really feel it's time we examined our feelings. I, for one, am convinced we're thoroughly suited to one another. Even before you left to come here, I was ready to make an announcement, and now, after forty-five days without you . . ."

Had he really been counting the days? He was right about one thing, at any rate. After all that time they should know their minds. She had given herself the same arguments several times, and had never been able to make a final commitment. But—

"I love you. I think we ought to get married."

There it was. He had proposed just at the moment when she felt the least able to think coherently.

"Howard," she began tentatively, "you're right about it being time to examine our feelings. It's just that, with my father's death and the sudden problems I'm facing with the *Star*, I really haven't had a chance to think about anything except my current situation." Which then included a reawakening of her feelings for Gary, feelings that—after his remarks on the dock—she'd begun to realize might not be reciprocated.

"I'd hoped that being apart would solidify your thoughts concerning our relationship. It certainly did mine. I don't want to be away from you again, Marilee. I want us to be together, always."

The speech was as close to being romantic as Howard ever got, and she felt a rush of tenderness toward him for having made such an admission. He was a very dear, sweet, intelligent . . . friend . . . a description she knew he would not want to hear.

As if accepting her silence as agreement, he rushed on eagerly, touching her arm and leaning close to her. "We have to do it soon. I don't want to wait any longer, Mare."

Surprised, Marilee looked up at him. He never shortened her name, didn't believe in nicknames. That was too casual for Howard. Only Gary had done that, so many years before when he had taken to calling her Lee.

"Howard, please. Let me get my breath. This is a little . . . surprising."

"Is it?" His gaze grew even more serious. "I thought you were aware of how deeply I care about you."

"Yes, but—"

"I love you."

"Oh." She could think of nothing else to say.

"Well." Howard cleared his throat. "Now that we have that clearly established, I really feel the time has come, Marilee. I almost proposed to you the week before you came out here, but then I put it off again. I must admit I've had some doubts—about myself, not about you," he added hastily, "about whether I was ready to settle down and accept all the responsibilities of marriage. But your being away cleared up my uncertainty once and for all, and made me realize how much you mean to me." He captured her hand again.

She wanted to pull away, but the thought of hurting his feelings changed her mind. If only she could have anticipated this confession when she found him waiting on the dock. She might have been able to sidetrack him before he'd delivered his very well thought out, very serious proposal. But it was too late for that.

"Howard," she began slowly, "everything you've said is true. I've thought about you and me over these past few months, before I came here, that is. I want to be fair with you, as well as to myself, and, under the circumstances, you're going to have to give me more time."

"How much time? How much longer do you expect to remain here? Maybe I should take my vacation now and stay here on Eleuthera with you."

"No," she said quickly. Eleuthera was far too small an island to contain both Howard and Gary. "No, don't stay. I'll have to return to California by the fifteenth in any event. That's only a week or so away. We'll talk about it then." Before he could object, she stood up and retrieved her bag from where she'd deposited it in an empty chair.

"But what about now?" Howard rose too and stood facing her, his eyes pleading. "What am I supposed to do? I just got here. I need to see you."

"I'll see you tomorrow." She felt drained of emotion. All she wanted to do was get away to a quiet place, alone, where she could begin to make some sense out of everything that had happened to her.

"Shall I stay or go? Really, Marilee, I've come all this way—"

"I know, and I'm terribly sorry." She touched his arm gently, then withdrew it hurriedly, lest he attempt to pull her into another embrace. She couldn't, she simply couldn't bear to have him hold her, not now. "Howard, I don't mean to be unkind, but I really think it would be better if you went back to California and waited for me there."

"Then you will come back and marry me?"

"I didn't say that." Her voice dropped to a whisper. "I'll think about it, I really will." Again she tried to leave, and he restrained her.

"There won't be a plane out again until tomorrow afternoon. Suppose you think about it tonight, and we can discuss it again in the morning?"

She found herself agreeing. It was the least she could do after all the trouble he had put himself through.

"You will think about it seriously, won't you?"

"Of course I will." She forced a smile, patted his arm again, and then turned and left.

She crossed the gravel parking lot to the ancient Jeep, pulled open the door forcefully, and threw her purse into the adjacent seat. Why, oh, why had it happened just then? It was all she could think of as she drove back to where the *Star* lay in her berth.

Hurriedly, she walked toward the yacht. At the gangplank she thought of Gary, the way he always stepped over the railing instead of lifting it. His image intruded again when she crossed the stern, under the sunshade, suddenly remembering the day she had gotten even with him by dropping the ice cube down his shirt front. In the galley she was almost overwhelmed by the memory of his kissing her that very morning.

She sat down on the step. The bow below, the tiny cabins each of them had slept in, and the shower stall both had used, mocked her. She could never go down there again without remembering. Howard was forgotten already. There was no Howard in her life anymore. There was only Gary.

Her head on her knees, she fought back the tears. Her heart seemed ready to burst inside her chest. Was it possible she had fallen in love with Gary again, after all?

Chapter Sixteen

The beach was obscured by a fine gray mist. Dark rain clouds gathered across the sky, blotting out the sun and sending a chill through Marilee's body. She stood at the water's edge, with Gary holding her left hand, and Howard her right, each pulling her in opposite directions. As he gave her a litany of what their life together would be like, Howard's face bore the same earnest look it usually did. Gary laughed. She tried to plead with them to let her go, but the words stuck in her throat. Suddenly the sound of footsteps pounded in her ears. Someone was coming to rescue her. She sat upright in bed, and the last of the dream receded. She was not on the beach but aboard the *Southern Star,* and the footsteps were only someone walking along the dock.

For a moment she felt disoriented. When had she come into the room and gone to bed? Then her memory returned in a sudden rush. The night before, she had spent a frenzied three hours cleaning everything belowdecks, finally removing all of her belongings from the bow and storing them once more in the master stateroom. The hard work she gave her muscles, although intended to keep her mind from replaying scenes with Gary and Howard, only added to her confusion instead of clarifying her feelings for the two men.

What was worse, now that reality had come with the dawn, a serious financial problem confronted her. The check from the Wellmans had bounced, and she was left with the prospect of other bounced checks and—at the very least—a sullied reputation in the area. Her meager savings—strained already by the two-month leave she'd taken from her job—would be completely wiped out long before she repaid the bills she incurred on behalf of the cruise for the Wellmans. She still thought of her former guests under that name and hoped the authorities in Nassau would soon contact her with news of their capture. For all she knew, they could be deep in the heart of Timbuktu by now.

She fought down her anger at having been so ill-used and pushed aside the sheet. She climbed out of bed and took a quick shower, then dressed in long, white duck pants, a navy- and red-striped T-shirt, and white low-heeled sandals. Restless, still caught along the edges of the dream, she ran a comb distractedly through her hair. Stopping in the galley only long enough to brew a pot of fresh coffee and make two slices of toast, she took the pot, the toast, and a thick white mug upstairs to the saloon.

Seated in a comfortable chair, she sipped the coffee and ate part of a slice of toast before pushing the plate away. That morning her stomach was anything but receptive to food, which was not unexpected given her anxious state of mind. Less than a mile down the road, Howard was waiting at the Royal for her answer to his proposal.

Well, Lee, she asked herself, what exactly are you going to do about him? She realized at once that she had referred to herself by the special name Gary had given her. No one else, not even her father, had ever used it. But it was not the romantic, sentimental Lee she needed to call upon now, but cool, practical, cautious Marilee. Whatever she decided that morning, the rest of her life might well depend on it, and she owed it to Howard and to herself to give his proposal very serious thought.

The pad and pencil the Wellmans had used to keep their gin rummy score—or whatever they had been doing at the table, which she doubted now was a game—lay there still, and she pulled them toward her. In large, bold letters, she wrote Howard's name across the top. Then she drew a line down the center and on one side wrote *pro* and on the other *con*. It was almost like making out a shopping list, she decided with a twinge of guilt, and just about as dispassionate.

It was also what Howard might do under the circumstances, or perhaps had done before he had come to the definite conclusion that he wanted her for his wife.

She leaned back in her chair and sipped the strong, black coffee. A clear-cut image of Howard, standing on the dock in a business suit, came to her, and she had to smile at the memory. How completely out of place he had looked. But then, to be fair, she had to admit that a tropical island in the Atlantic Ocean was hardly his milieu. His was an air-conditioned office crammed with legal tomes, located over an hour, by freeway, from the nearest body of water.

She drew a heavy black line under Howard's name. Then her gaze moved down to where she had written the word *pro*. She stared at the blank space underneath and called to mind everything about Howard she had always admired.

He was intelligent, conscientious, and made more than an adequate living as a corporate lawyer. A plus for any man. He taught a course at UCLA and gave an occasional lecture before the California Bar Association. If he stayed with Mathiesen and Bellows, and she had no reason to think he wouldn't, within the next ten years he could, quite possibly, be made a partner. Of course, his earning power was not the most important consideration, nor had it ever influenced her decision to date Howard in the first place. Even now, faced with a situation that cried out for more resources than she had, she couldn't consider that a reason for choosing him.

What she had been drawn to most when they met was the obvious fact that he was dependable and reliable. What Gary wouldn't make of that. She jotted down the words, along with *considerate, kind, even-tempered,* and *punctual.* And they did have a few things in common. Both liked the symphony and attended concerts at the Hollywood Bowl, but they never went to any of the comedy showcases in Los Angeles, which she had once or twice hinted they try.

As she peered down at the list, she saw that it had grown considerably on the positive side, and she shifted her attention across to the negative. The empty space seemed to leap off the paper at her, and, deliberately, she set her mind to an honest assessment of Howard's shortcomings. Finally, after what seemed too long a time, she wrote one word, *stuffy,* and underlined it three times.

She frowned. Was that it? She brought her mug to her lips, sipping slowly. Strangely enough, she'd never really thought of him that way, or maybe she had and kept the thought pushed well back in her subconscious.

Stuffy. Yes, that summarized Howard, all right. The one word seemed to say it all.

She snapped the pad shut, pushed herself out of the chair, and crossed the saloon, gazing out of a starboard porthole. Howard, for all his qualities and seeming lack of faults, receded and she thought of Gary, making a mental list such as she had just made on paper.

With him, a different set of words came to mind: *exciting, provocative, impetuous, bold*—the list went on and on. Not that it mattered. She had made her decision about Gary eight years before, and even if she were to change her mind, he was not about to offer her the chance.

Okay, she wouldn't change her mind. She'd forget him.

"Ahoy there," a voice called from the dock. She recognized Jane Owens. "Do you have a minute?"

Marilee crossed to the porthole and waved Jane aboard.

"I hope you don't mind my barging in like this," Jane said, entering the saloon. "I didn't expect to find you up this early."

A weak smile pulled at Marilee's mouth. "I've gotten used to it these past ten days." She remembered the mornings she rose early to get breakfast ready for everyone and to help Gary organize the fishing and snorkeling gear.

"I was just down at the end of the dock," Jane said. "I thought I saw you in here." She glanced around as if she almost expected someone else to be there. "Are you sure you don't mind if I come in and chat for a few minutes?"

"No, not at all." Marilee made a staunch attempt to hide her lack of enthusiasm. Usually she welcomed a visit from Jane, who always seemed to be upbeat and cheerful, but not that morning when she was faced with having to repeat bad news and was caught in an emotional tug-of-war besides. "Would you like some coffee? I'll get you a mug."

"No, thanks." Jane held up a restraining hand and settled into a chair. "How was the cruise?"

"Fine," Marilee said, taking the opposite seat, not able to keep some sarcasm out of her voice, "except for one little thing. The Wellmans, which is not really their names, are wanted in three states for embezzling and check fraud and yours truly is their latest victim."

"What?" Jane almost rose from her chair. "I don't understand. What happened?"

Marilee made the ugly story as brief as possible, ending with the assurance that, although the local check she had given to Jane might come back from the bank, she was prepared to offer her another—definitely cash-worthy—from her California account.

"I'm not worried about *my* money." Jane scoffed. "But you, just when you thought you had enough to stave off the bank for a while. What will you do now?"

Marilee sighed wearily. "First, I have to call the bank, and everyone to whom I wrote checks before we left on the cruise, and assure them I'll make good on what I owe. As for the *Star,* well, there's still a little time to find a buyer. I'll have to call Mike. Maybe he's found one already and my problems will be over."

"What about Gary Pritchard?"

"Oh, he'll get paid too . . . somehow." Marilee didn't want to talk about Gary, or even think about him, because it only reminded her how much he was influencing her decision about Howard.

"The food was out of this world," she told Jane, to change the subject. "The compliments I received belong to you. The dinner service was a snap. All I did was heat and serve what you had already prepared. Which reminds me. I was going to stop at your house this morning and return the containers, but—" She stopped short.

"But?" Jane prompted.

"Something came up," Marilee evaded.

Jane propped her elbows on the table and leaned closer. "Would it have anything to do with the well-dressed man who was looking frantically for you yesterday?"

Marilee nodded. She didn't want to explain Howard to Jane, or his reasons for appearing so suddenly on Eleuthera. "He finally caught up with me as we were pulling into the dock," was the only answer she felt ready to give.

Then abruptly she changed the subject again. "I have all the containers washed and stacked in the galley. If you'd like to take them with you today, I'll get them."

As she began to rise, Jane held her off. "There's no rush." She settled comfortably in the chair. "I really came on board to gossip."

Marilee looked over in time to catch a spark of mischief in Jane's eyes, but couldn't head her off.

"Between this Madison Avenue type," Jane went on, "rushing around looking for you, dressed as if he were about to conduct a board meeting, and Gary looking like a ton of bricks had fallen on him, I thought something interesting might be in the wind." She paused for breath. "I wondered if I could wheedle it out of you." She smiled a conspirator's smile and waited for an answer.

A short silence settled. Then Marilee said, "I don't know what you mean. Howard is an old and dear friend from California. He didn't know anything about the cruise and was worried about not finding me here. As for Gary, there's no reason why he should look as if he'd been hit with a brick." If anyone had the right to look like that, Marilee reasoned, after what had occurred during the past two days alone, it was she.

"I thought that was unlike him, although I admit I haven't seen him much since he came back to Eleuthera. But it seemed strange, all the same, for him to return from a ten-day cruise with a beautiful woman and look like someone just stole his teddy bear."

Gary looking forlorn? No way. Even if he felt like that, no one would ever suspect. "I think you misinterpreted the look," Marilee said. She rose from her chair, stretched her arms, and walked to the open porthole. "If anything, the situation is probably just the opposite."

"Now what does *that* mean? You're as elusive as him."

Marilee whirled around. "What did you ask him? What did he say?" As quickly as the words spilled out, she regretted them. It would only add to her devastation if another person knew of her feelings for Gary, feelings, she was certain, were not reciprocated.

"He wouldn't say anything, told me to ask you. Can I help it if I'm too old to have a romance myself and keep looking for it among you young people? You're single, Gary's single, you go off on a cruise together for ten days and come back looking unhappy. Even if the Wellmans did cause a problem, financially and otherwise, it shouldn't change how you two feel about each other. You're ruining my notion of how things ought to turn out. I'll have to go back to reading paperback novels from the drugstore again."

"I'm afraid life isn't much like novels," Marilee said slowly. "And I'm sorry if we destroyed your illusions. In the first place, we had less free time than you might imagine. Besides cooking and housekeeping, there were a hundred other jobs to do trying to make the cruise enjoyable for the Wellmans, who actually deserved to be in the hold of a slave ship. When there was any free time, I was too pooped to enjoy it. And in the second place—" She stopped. She could not lay bare her emotional distress, even to so good and dear a friend as Jane. Anyway, it would do no good. She turned to face the scene outside the porthole, too late to hide her telltale look of regret.

Jane rose and went over to where Marilee stood. "I think I just managed to put my big foot into my even bigger mouth." After a pause, she said, "Is something wrong?"

Everything is wrong, Marilee told the woman silently, but she couldn't bring herself to say it aloud.

"Things have gotten a little confused," she conceded. "They'll sort themselves out eventually." She wished she could believe that, but knew she was no longer that naive.

"Would you like to tell me about it?" Jane touched Marilee lightly on the arm. "In spite of my mouth running away with me at times, I'm a good listener. Often that's what a person needs most, to have someone else to talk to."

"There's really nothing to be concerned about." Marilee's laugh had a false ring to it. "I just need some time to be by myself, to make some decisions."

She glanced toward the clock. "I told Howard I'd drive him back to the airport today," she said idly, almost as if Jane were no longer there. "He's waiting at the Royal."

"Mare." Jane sounded worried. "I don't want you to think I'm prying, or that I enjoy sticking my nose in where it doesn't belong, but if you decide you'd like someone to talk to, you can always find me."

Marilee gave Jane a brief hug. "I know."

Jane turned to leave. "Don't forget."

"I won't."

When Marilee was alone, she retrieved the pad and removed the single piece of paper on which she'd been writing. She studied it carefully before folding it neatly in half, then in halves again, until it became a very small square. Then she dropped it in an ashtray, struck a match, and waited until the small wad of paper turned to gray ash.

Chapter Seventeen

Marilee left the *Star* and walked over to the office of South Wind Charters. She opened the windows as wide as possible and let the sweet smell of the sea waft indoors, but the mound of bills and other necessary paperwork that had multiplied during her absence would not be as easy to eliminate as the stale, shut-up odors.

Before seating herself at the desk, she gathered up the new mail and hurriedly sorted through it, separating it into two piles: correspondence she needed to address immediately and that which looked unimportant. The latter hit the wastebasket, as there was no point in filing anything away in the metal cabinet that eventually must be sold to the secondhand dealer, along with the other office equipment, desk, chairs, tables, and framed maps of the Bahamas.

With a patience she would not have believed possible two weeks before, she went through every scrap of paper, old or new, that required her attention and handled it at once, finally realizing that it would take less time

145

to do it immediately than put it aside and return to it later.

Tapping the keys of her father's outdated but still useful computer, she wrote letters first, apologizing for the bad checks and enclosing new ones written on her California account. Although her balance had dwindled considerably, she couldn't let those remain unpaid. Then she methodically sorted the other bills into the order of importance. The *Star* came first and she wrote a check for one overdue payment. Score one for the bank. Second came Jane's bill. But the money ran out before she went any further in the stack. Then she thought of Gary again. He, too, must be paid. But with what? Twice he'd said she needn't pay him: once when he'd squashed her chance to sell the *Star* to the Clarks and again when they learned the Wellmans' check had bounced. But that didn't change her mind. Her problems were not his problems; it was she who had decided to honor her father's commitment, not Gary. She didn't resent her dad, but wished he hadn't left her to deal with this.

She composed a terse, professional note informing Gary that she would pay for his services in installments as soon as she returned to California and began earning a regular paycheck again. Then she wrote his name and address on a small white envelope and, placing a stamp in the corner, she deposited it on the corner of the desk, in front of the other letters she had written.

At the sight of his name on the envelope, a feeling of weakness threatened to wash over her and tear down her hastily constructed defenses. Memories flooded in on her of when she was a teenager and had first fallen head over heels in love with him. In those days she had written the name Gary Pritchard over many a page in her school notebooks, especially in the first few days after returning to her studies. Gradually, the need to verify his existence in permanent ink subsided, and only occasionally thereafter, as the school year progressed, would she feel the need to write out his name, until eventually, in an occasional bout of neatness, she would throw away all such reminders of him in an orgy of straightening her room or desk. Only to begin the ritual again the following year.

She sighed, rose from the desk, gathered the letters, and tucked them into her purse before leaving the office.

When she walked out of the airport two hours later, something inside felt free, as if she were a bird who had just learned how to fly. Bits and pieces of her conversation with Howard floated in her consciousness. Their farewell began with his urging her to return to California with him that very day.

She'd protested that, since the cruise had dashed her hopes to continue making payments on the *Star,* she had to sell the yacht more urgently than ever and she still had another week to accomplish it.

To Marilee's way of thinking, however, the worst part of the conversation was convincing Howard not to wait for her. That when she returned to California, it would be for her job and nothing more.

He'd surprised her by suggesting she had fallen in love with Eleuthera Island again. It wasn't like Howard to be so perceptive. And it wasn't just the island, but memories of her father and how close they'd been. Now, when she and Howard had said good-bye and his plane was no longer even a tiny speck in the cloudless sky, she felt he was completely convinced at last her answer to his proposal was an unequivocal no.

She'd been convincing herself as much as him, she realized. Even if she never saw Gary again, she was right not to marry dear, conventional, predictable Howard. She knew at last she had too much of her father in her for that. Most of all, she would never forgive herself if she married Howard, when it was so obvious that her heart lay elsewhere.

She sighed deeply. Her disturbing dream, her talks with Jane and Howard had all exacted a toll on her nerves. She longed to get off by herself and sort out her thoughts about Gary. She remembered what Jane had said about his dour look when she'd seen him. Had she misinterpreted that look, and if not, did it have anything to do with Howard's appearance on Eleuthera? Could Gary Pritchard actually be jealous? She pondered that as she walked across the terminal toward the parking lot.

Then she changed her mind. She didn't want to drive anywhere just then. By the time she was seated in the terminal coffee shop, she had already dismissed the notion of Gary's jealousy. Just thinking back over his droll remarks at the dock the day before was enough to convince her that his feelings didn't run in that direction. Not for a moment did he seem to take Howard seriously, and if he felt any emotion at all, it was most likely because he viewed Howard not as serious competition, but as an annoying intrusion.

She had barely seated herself in a booth and ordered some iced tea when Gary himself sauntered up. Without a word but with a devilish smile on his face, he slipped in across from her and set his glass on the table. Then he stretched his bare arms across the back of the seat, giving every indication he was planning to stay for awhile.

"What are you doing here?" The words spilled out before she could stop them.

"I was sending a set of drawings to my partner in Nassau and decided to stop in for a cool drink before driving back. I'm sorry if my appearance upsets you."

"It doesn't upset me," she answered hurriedly. "I'm just, er, surprised, that's all." The reasons he gave for being in the area made no impression in her mind. Her only concern was that she wasn't ready to speak to him yet. A long pause sent her gaze into her lap, where she smoothed out the fold in her napkin.

"You're here too," he commented, breaking the silence.

"Yes." Would he wonder why? Would he even care? Oh, where was that rapport they'd enjoyed so recently? How could it have eroded with the end of the cruise, like a candle flame extinguished in the wind?

"Seeing Howard off, were you?"

"As a matter of fact, yes," she said softly.

"Are you going to marry him?"

At the words, her gaze flew to his face and in a louder tone she answered, "That's none of your business!"

His deep-throated laugh echoed in the room and turned the heads of some other patrons. Gary lowered his voice, but the mocking tone remained. "You've been wanting to convince yourself he's the right man, haven't you?"

When Marilee didn't answer, he continued. "The last ten days should have done that. Or do you want someone to make the decision for you, Lee?" He leaned forward, resting his arms on the table. "Well, no one can do that. But if you're looking for someone who will never ruffle your feathers, someone who will make each day as predictable as the last, then Howard ought to look very good to you now."

Another pause. Marilee felt something akin to beating wings, like flocks of angry birds, inside her body.

"No matter," Gary said with a shrug, letting one long finger glide over the smooth wood of the tabletop. "Not that you and I can't be friends. But I'm sure Howard can offer more than that."

Marilee's thoughts flew to her morning scribbling, writing down Howard's attributes and thinking about Gary's. It was almost as if Gary had caught her at it.

"He's so . . . how would you describe him?" He leaned closer. "Conservative, certainly."

"Is that a crime?"

"Not at all like me," he went on. "And settled nicely into the legal profession. That was obvious from the three-piece Italian suit."

"You are infuriating!" Marilee managed in a low, choked voice. Why was he torturing her that way? Why couldn't he just come right out and tell her if he cared or not?

"Now, Lee," he cajoled. "I'm not criticizing the man.

I'm merely reminding you of his good points, the orderly, predictable life he can provide. I can't have you miss out on it now that Mister Reliable has chased you clear across the continent."

"His qualities are no concern of yours." Marilee could hardly breathe. It was like déjà vu. They had had a similar discussion in Gary's house the day she'd asked him to skipper the *Star.* But in the days afterward, so much had happened. Did that mean nothing to him?

"I can see it now," Gary continued, crossing one long leg over the other, ankle to knee. "You'll be married in June, of course. That's the traditional month for weddings and Howard will want to be traditional, I have no doubt. You'll buy a split-level house in the suburbs, not too far from the office—he wouldn't want his commute to last longer than the network news—but in a really good part of town. On weekends, there'll be shopping at the mall, or a quiet dinner at your favorite restaurant."

She raised her voice. "Gary—"

"And you'll have two children, a boy and a girl, naturally. Good old dependable Howard surely has some way of arranging that!"

"Gary!"

"You'll quit your job, as soon as the kids arrive. His wife shouldn't work. Good-bye job, hello, dullsville. No ad-libbing through life for you two."

He paused, as if expecting a retort from her, but her mind had gone numb with the accurate way he voiced all her fears about the kind of life she might have with Howard.

"You'll entertain once a month at dinner parties for

eight—his business associates and their wives—and the conversations will be about finding good private schools, corporate infighting, and which politician is conservative enough for you."

"I'm not going to sit here and listen to this."

Suddenly his mood changed. He leaned back against the seat and ran a hand through his thick, glossy hair. "I'm through, Lee. You don't need me to tell you these things, anyway. You know them well enough yourself."

"And just what is that supposed to mean?"

"Lee, that's not you. I tried to tell you that years ago, but you wouldn't listen."

"You don't really know me or anything about me," she threw at him. "You don't have the slightest idea how I feel or how I think. You hadn't seen me in eight years before the cruise."

He laughed briefly. "I have all the credentials where you're concerned. Remember, Lee, I watched you grow up. From a pig-tailed urchin who followed her father around like a worshipful slave, to an intelligent, resourceful, desirable woman."

Warmth stole into her cheeks at the sudden memory of just how desirable she had seemed to him that day at the beach. There had been no mistaking the desire in his eyes, in his every action. But nothing had come of it.

"You're as adventurous as your father. Every marriage needs a little mystery, and you'd get none of that with Howard. You don't fit into his lifestyle, and no matter how hard you try, you never will. You know it."

"Maybe I'm more like him than you think. I'm not that pig-tailed child who dogged my father's footsteps.

I teach networking systems to people. I'm a serious businesswoman."

"That doesn't make you an automaton. Part of you loves the precision of the work, loves the challenge to pass on your knowledge to others. I can understand that. But another part of you longs for adventure, the unexpected."

He was too close to the mark, as if he could look into her very soul. But she couldn't let him know. "And just where has your adventurous nature gotten you?"

His eyes changed, a soft, tender quality crept in. "It's gotten me you."

"You never had me."

A wicked smile settled on his lips. "Let's not be technical. In the end, it's brought you here to me."

"I came here because of my father's death. I have to sell the *Star* and pay his debts. It had absolutely nothing to do with you."

He continued on as if she hadn't spoken. "And when you needed a skipper for the cruise, you turned to me. Was that what you wanted all along, Lee? Did you want to see me again? Maybe one last time in order to compare me to Howard? If so, I'm glad you did."

"That's not true." But of course he was right. Now that he had said it aloud, it was all too clear that had been her intent all along. She had convinced herself she had to honor the last cruise on the printed schedule, but the truth was no one would have expected her to do that after her father's death. And look what anguish *that* decision had brought down on her.

Now, in hindsight, she realized she should have

cancelled the cruise, tried harder to find a buyer for the *Star,* or accepted the bank's auction. But what she should never have done was gone near Gary Pritchard.

"You haven't answered my question. Are you going to marry Howard?"

How she longed to say no, but the triumph in his eyes would devastate her. Still, she couldn't let him think she could react to his many kisses as she had, and then fly back to the West Coast a week later to marry someone else. Didn't he know she wouldn't do that? Didn't he sense that their time together had rekindled her feelings for him?

His voice softened again. "You think you're like your mother. You think that, like her, you need security of the walk-in-the-door-at-six-p.m., paycheck-every-Friday kind. But there's more of your father in you than you realize. If Howard had been right for you, you'd have married him long ago. You know that as well as I do. I hope you finally cut him loose."

Once more she couldn't answer. She could not say yes anymore than she could say no before. But would he read her answer in her silence? Where was his clairvoyance when she needed it?

Suddenly, he drained his drink. "I apologize, Lee. I've been out of line again. You're twenty-six years old. You don't need me to tell you how to lead your life. You obviously know what you want." He stood up. "Well, we both have things to do, I'm sure. I put my business on hold for ten days, and it's time I got back to it."

Marilee pulled the envelope from her purse and held it out. Since she would never see him again, she had to give it to him then. "I hope you didn't think I'd forgotten about paying you for the cruise. Unfortunately, there's no check in here. Just my promise to pay you when the *Star* is sold or after I get back to work, whichever comes first."

For some seconds, he stared at her before extending his hand to take it. Then his gaze dropped and seemed to rest on the uncancelled stamp in the corner, but he made no comment. Without opening the envelope, he dropped it on the table. "You don't have to pay me at all. You have enough financial obligations without that."

"You worked hard, you deserve to be paid too." He didn't answer and she was disturbed by the awkward silence, but could think of no way to break it. She sipped from her glass, trying to moisten her desert-dry throat.

He sat down again, spread one arm across the back of the booth and looked across at her. "When do you return to California?"

"The week after next." She wondered why it seemed a natural question. Was he anxious for her to leave or hoping she'd stay? Would he say anything at all to let her know his feelings? "My two-month leave will be up by then. I'll have to return to my job whether I've sold the *Star* or not."

"No buyers yet?"

She glanced out the window and watched a small plane starting to taxi down the runway. "Not a one. You wouldn't care to buy her yourself, would you?" She put a light laugh into her voice, then turned serious. "Can you use another yacht in your charter service, or is the *Seafarer* enough?"

He ignored her question. After a long pause, he said, "I'm afraid I didn't behave very well a little while ago. As you so rightly informed me, what you do about Howard is none of my business. I'm sorry. I hope you'll accept my apology." And then he was gone.

She tried to pay her bill, but found Gary had done that. She drove back slowly, wondering what to do next.

Gary had summed it all up neatly, but he had left the most important question unanswered. Where did that leave her? He had suggested that she knew her own mind. So why was she more confused than ever? The next logical question then was, what *did* she want? But there really was no need to ask. She'd known the answer from the moment she saw him standing in front of his house in Governor's Harbor. At last she forced herself to admit it. What she wanted now and would always want was what she had foolishly thrown away eight years before: Gary Pritchard.

Chapter Eighteen

After a brief stop at the *Star* for Jane's food containers, Marilee got into the Jeep again and drove to Jane's cottage. She was met with the usual invitation to have a cup of tea and homemade goodies.

Jane put two teaspoons of tea into a china pot and added boiling water. "Shall we sit outside in the garden?" She gathered up cups, saucers, plates, and silverware.

Marilee followed her outside to a circular glass-topped table shaded by a green umbrella and flanked by four white wrought-iron chairs.

While Marilee arranged the china, Jane went inside, returning a moment later with a mouth-watering pineapple pie and the teapot.

Marilee poured the tea while Jane slid a generous slice of pie onto each plate.

"Will you still be going back to California when your two-month leave is up?" Jane tipped the umbrella, further shading the area where they sat.

"I had never considered staying beyond that. In fact,"

she said, after a pause, "it seems rather pointless not to go back right now."

"Is that what you want to do?"

Marilee didn't answer at once. It had been two days since Gary had left her in the coffee shop, their argument—if that's what it was—unfinished. They had been the most miserable two days of her life—worse than their parting eight years before—and she took them as a signal of what the rest of her stay on the island would be like.

"I'm not sure what I want," Marilee admitted honestly. "Maybe if I just went home . . ."

"Would that solve anything?" Jane asked gently. "You have a problem, and it's not just the money crunch, is it?"

"I've been worried about the *Star,*" Marilee said, half wanting to close the subject, but knowing deep inside she should confide in Jane.

"What's bothering you has nothing to do with a yacht. And if the hangdog look I've seen come into your eyes every now and then is any indication, I'd say the problem has something to do with Gary. That somehow the two of you had a misunderstanding. Take my advice and patch it up."

"If it were only that easy."

"Of course it's not," Jane agreed. "Not when you're in love with a man."

"You're mistaken," Marilee lied, her voice close to quavering. "There isn't anything between us."

In a barely discernible whisper, Jane said, "And the moon is made of green cheese."

Suddenly the futility of her petty deception swept over Marilee. "Is it that obvious?"

"To a person who's known you just about all your life, yes. Come on now, tell me what happened. I really want to help. We older people know a few things about life and love. I was married twice myself. The first ended in divorce, but the second, well, I'd rather stay a widow than try to find someone as sweet as that man."

Marilee leaned back in her chair and sighed deeply. "I appreciate your offer, but I don't think you can help. I don't think anyone can."

"If you love one another—"

"That's just the point," Marilee said. "Whatever Gary feels for me, I'm sure it isn't love. I think I'd be able to sense it." She had eight years earlier, before he'd ever admitted his feelings for her, before he had asked her to marry him that day aboard *Seafarer.* Now, older and more mature, could her judgment be that unsound?

"But you love him?"

Marilee laughed bitterly, over the irony of how it felt to have the shoe on the other foot. "Maybe I never stopped loving him."

"And how do you know it isn't reciprocated?" Jane asked kindly. "Did he tell you?"

Marilee picked up her fork and toyed with the edge of her pie. "Not in so many words. And maybe I deserve it. Maybe he's just playing a game with me, trying to make me fall in love with him again. But he's become inconsistent, as if neither the *Star* nor I exist any longer."

"Howard's appearance might have had something to do with that," Jane said. "You know, Marilee, no man, no matter how sure he is of a woman, welcomes competition. And don't ever believe a man who says he does."

Marilee let her gaze wander around the garden while she mulled that over. Could Howard have had that much of an effect on Gary's attitude, if any at all? She'd asked herself that earlier and had dismissed the idea then.

"I doubt that's the case," she said finally, glancing over at Jane. "By the time we docked back here, Gary already seemed detached. At least, I thought so at the time. Then he saw Howard kiss me."

"What did I tell you?" Jane scoffed. "Competition!"

"Gary can't be jealous. The day I said good-bye to Howard at the airport, Gary and I met by chance at the terminal coffee shop and he insulted Howard on the one hand, and tried to throw me at him on the other."

Jane was silent for a moment. Then she said, "All right, maybe he's not jealous. Maybe he's only giving you a little room. Time to examine your own feelings and make up your mind whether you want him or Howard. Good grief, the man has waited for you for eight years. It won't hurt him to wait a little bit longer."

Marilee shook her head. "You weren't there, you just don't understand." She pushed herself up from the chair and went out into the garden, where a circular pond held an assortment of brilliantly hued tropical fish. She watched them dart around in the water and wished her life were as peaceful and uncomplicated as theirs seemed to be.

She made a sudden decision. "I'm going to sell everything in the office now. There's no reason to keep any of it anymore." Her voice turned firm with a hint of sarcasm. "I won't be doing any more cruises with anyone."

"Don't be in such a hurry," Jane warned. "Give yourself and Gary time to work this out."

Time? At this rate, they'd both be too old to care if the relationship ever resolved itself.

"Time isn't going to make anything work out," she said. "Eight years didn't change anything, why should another few days?" She faced Jane, feeling none of the peace the garden should have generated.

"What's the number of the second-hand store? I'm going to have them cart everything out of that office tomorrow. By the next day I can be on a flight home. The sooner the better." Why had she ever thought she could stay on the same island with Gary any longer?

Jane went to her and took both of her hands. "Don't go home yet. Go to Gary. Tell him honestly how you feel."

"Jane, I can't. Gary would—" She stopped herself. What could she tell him? That she had fallen in love with him and hadn't the faintest idea whether or not that meant anything to him? These were modern times and she considered herself a contemporary woman, but not to the extent that she could make such an admission.

Or maybe she should admit that a man she liked and respected—and should have fallen in love with long before if she'd had any sense—had flown four thousand miles to ask her to marry him? And that she had turned him down. Would that amuse him or would it clear the air between them?

"What can you lose by talking honestly with him, a little pride? Stoke up your courage. Pride makes a very cold bed partner."

At the words, Marilee's face turned hot. "How does a woman tell a man 'I love you' when she has no idea how he feels about her? That takes more than courage. You'd have to be a lunatic. It's impossible."

Jane smiled. "You can be more subtle than that. Not too vague, mind you, or you'll never get it cleared up."

"Subtle or not, I can't."

"At least confront him." Jane was equally insistent. "Look at his face. That should tell you something. Some men have a terrible time hiding what they really feel. The worst he can do is tell you to go back to California. He won't kick you out physically, you know."

A momentary vision of Gary placing a well-aimed foot on her posterior made Marilee suddenly laugh. It felt good to laugh at herself, at anything. "I suppose not."

Then she was back in the doldrums again. "It won't work, and I'm not just being stubborn."

"I hope you change your mind. Like you did when you asked Gary to captain the *Star* for the cruise."

"This is different. Besides, it would have been better if I'd never asked him. Then I wouldn't have fallen in love with him again. And I wouldn't be in even worse financial trouble than I was before."

Jane patted her gently on the back. "That's beside the point. Do it. You really must, you know."

Marilee took a deep gulp of air, trying to calm herself. She trusted Jane, but— "I'll think about it."

"Good. Don't go back to California until you're absolutely sure there's nothing left for you here."

"Thanks, Jane. I can't promise, but I won't arbitrarily discount talking to Gary. I can't imagine what difference it will make, though."

"You're not afraid to take chances. If you were, you would have packed up and gone back to California with Howard."

As Marilee walked back to the Jeep, she knew Jane was right. But could she take that particular chance?

Chapter Nineteen

All that night and the next day, Marilee's thoughts focused on her meeting with Gary. Yet, their conversation didn't reflect any peaceful thoughts on his part. Were he punishing her deliberately, he could not have been more successful in making her miserable.

A throbbing pain began behind her eyelids. Many times she had wondered if he'd been seeking revenge and dismissed the notion. Even then, it was impossible to believe he could be so petty. He had obviously enjoyed their time together on the cruise, but apparently his feelings didn't extend to wanting it to last. She had gotten just what she deserved. Now she loved him and he was indifferent. She had once thrown away her opportunity for happiness with him, and he had shown her that he'd completely recovered from the hurt she'd inflicted on him. The knot in her stomach turned to a dull, persistent ache, and she knew it would last forever.

She left the *Star* and walked over to the office, entering the little building for what might be the last time. The furniture was gone, and it was an echoing, empty shell. So much for her disgusting efficiency in calling the second-hand store. A sprinkling of sand covered the bare wooden floor, and, in the corner, looking forlorn, stood the telephone. As she stared at it, tears stinging her eyes, it rang.

"I have a buyer for the *Southern Star.*" Mike's announcement on the other end of the line caught Marilee completely unaware. Her mind had been so preoccupied with Gary, that the *Star*—the very thing that had brought them back into each other's lives—had been relegated to the background.

She took a moment to compose herself. First, she wondered if she ought to be skeptical. Mike had said that to her once before and it turned out not to be true. Gary had admitted he'd scuttled the sale that other time, but now she was fairly certain that it had somehow been Mike's fault and Gary simply took the blame to shield his friend. She knew Gary well enough now to know he was capable of that kind of gesture. But confronting Mike with the truth would do no good. If a legitimate buyer had come forward to keep the bank from repossessing the yacht, Mike deserved praise, not censure.

"That's good news, Mike. Who's buying her?"

"Some outfit over in Nassau wants it for public relations purposes. I spoke to a man by the name of Steve Johnson. He's apparently an attorney, prepared to negotiate fully on behalf of his clients. I gather there's more than one of them. He said he knew your father some and had heard a lot about the *Star.*"

She thought for a moment. "The name isn't familiar

to me, but that doesn't mean anything." Her father had friends on so many of the islands, she was bound to be unfamiliar with some of them. She sat down on the bare wooden floor, wishing she had the old leather swivel chair. Yet, the hardness really made little impression on her. Her mind was still digesting the news that she would soon no longer own the *Southern Star.* It had been in her father's possession so long, she couldn't remember anything before it.

"Is he coming to inspect the *Star?*"

"No, he remembers her well, and of course I showed him recent pictures. He said he knew your dad always kept the vessel in top condition."

Marilee didn't comment, and Mike continued. "He wants to conclude all of the arrangements as soon as possible. It's one of the conditions."

"That's no problem. Since I'm due to return to California in a few days, I'm just as anxious as he is."

"And," Mike continued, "he's willing to pay the price you asked, no dickering at all."

The full price! "That's even better news. When does he want to come over here to pick her up and sign the papers?"

"Well, that's another condition," Mike went on, "but with the favorable terms he was offering, I didn't think you'd mind. He wants you to deliver the yacht to him in Nassau day after tomorrow. Meantime, he'll put the money in escrow."

"Why Nassau? Why can't he pick her up here?" She wondered how she was going to deliver the *Star* to him.

"Says he can't spare the time to fly over here right

now, and since he's paying top dollar, and I know how anxious you are to sell, I didn't think you'd want me to argue the point."

"No," she conceded. "You're right. I can just as easily fly back to Eleuthera or take the boat if necessary. I'm not in any position to bargain. I can't afford to wait around for another buyer, even if I thought we'd find one."

"So, shall I tell him you're agreeable?" Mike asked.

"Yes."

"I'll get the necessary papers drawn up and have them ready for you tomorrow. You can take them with you when you run the *Star* over to Nassau."

"Thanks, Mike. I really appreciate your help. This solves so many of my problems."

"As you know, I advertised extensively. But when this fellow called and said he would buy the *Star* on your terms, I could have sent him a kiss over the wire."

Marilee laughed with him at the mental image of the heavyset, bearded Mike going to such an extreme.

After she put down the phone, she continued to sit on the floor, alternately pleased and disappointed. She had to sell the *Star* but wished she didn't. That was a ridiculous fantasy. Even if she'd been able to keep her, she would never again return to Eleuthera. That chapter in her life had closed for good. Soon Gary would be only a memory, an aching for something that could never be.

Still, memories of the cruise and their last day together in Nassau rushed at her. Although the temperature spiked into the eighties, shivers raced up her skin. She tried not to think of never seeing him again, but he'd been right. She *was* more like her father. She loved the islands, understood the lure of the sea, and needed to be even a small part of the life that surrounded it. But she could never have that with Gary back on Eleuthera. Being so close to him—without having him love her—was impossible.

With difficulty, she turned her thoughts to the *Southern Star*. She had to deliver her to Nassau but could hardly do that by herself. She would have to ask Gary to help her once more.

Gary. A spark of hope ignited again. Perhaps, with the realization that she would leave at week's end, he would give some indication of his feelings. As Jane had suggested, she needed to see him once more and find out for certain. He openly enjoyed her company, and in Nassau she had made her own feelings obvious. They had become more than just old friends, and a closeness had grown between them. How then could he feel nothing? She had to know one way or the other what he felt about her. She could make it happen when they were alone on the *Star*, or even in Nassau.

A smile crept over her face. She'd been given a perfect opportunity: the new owner wanted the *Star* delivered to him. This time she wouldn't let her pride stand in the way. She wouldn't wait for him to declare his love for her first. How could she have let those precious days go by without telling him how she felt? That was all over. As Jane had said, pride made a cold bed partner, even in the Bahamas.

With her business completed in Nassau, they'd be alone. She'd tell him he had only to say the word and she'd never leave; she'd stay and be near him forever. The very thought sent her heart catapulting into her throat. She just had to hope he'd captain her yacht one more time. She picked up the phone to call him.

Chapter Twenty

Gary's greeting as he came on board the yacht two days later was reminiscent of the last time they'd been together. He seemed friendly, even kissed her on the cheek with some eagerness. But as much pleasure as she found in his touch, there was no denying reality.

For all her wild imagining of a scene in Nassau when she would shamelessly admit she didn't want to live without him, the fact was he had never even hinted that he loved her, or that he wanted their new relationship to develop further. She hated herself for the ambivalence of her feelings—hope one minute, despair the next. The last was strongest today, the belief that, to him, their meeting was nothing more than a brief encounter. No doubt he considered her someone out of his checkered past, a woman he had once loved and proposed to but who meant nothing to him now.

He stepped back. "Maybe we'd better get under way."

"I suppose you're right. Mr. Johnson expects me at his office before five today."

"It's only a six-hour trip," he reminded her. "We'll be there on time."

"I know, but I don't want anything to go wrong with this sale. It's too important to me."

She plunged down the steps to the galley, her mind rehearsing again the moment she would tell him her feelings, that is, if her nerve didn't fail her. She busied herself by putting away the lunch she'd brought on board, made coffee, and brought it up to Gary. He was sitting in the cockpit marking navigation charts when she approached.

"We'll come around Spanish Wells and continue southwest, off the coast of Current Island," he said, showing her the route. "Then we'll head due west and make straight for Nassau."

She leaned toward the chart, listening, following the lines carefully with her eyes, then handed him his coffee.

"Will you miss the *Star?*" He accepted the mug, making no reference to their previous conversation.

She nodded. "I have a lot of good memories. We met aboard the *Star,* if I remember correctly." She looked directly at him.

"Did we?" He looked away. "I guess so."

Could he have sounded any more disinterested? She sipped her coffee slowly, hardly tasting it. When Gary started the engines and told her to get ready to cast off, she gulped down the last of it and then leaped easily to the dock, where she loosened the fore and aft lines for their departure.

When the *Star* was out of the harbor at last and headed for Nassau, she went below. It was cool and windy topside, with an unusually overcast sky, not the sunny day she was accustomed to, so she didn't feel too deprived spending her time preparing the *Star* for its new owners.

On the previous day, she had stripped the linens from the bunks and removed all items from their storage places, in addition to the personal belongings she had brought on board. She had filled box after box with linens, blankets and towels, dishes, pots and pans, silverware, and glasses. Then there were more boxes of books, games, and puzzles that her father always provided for his clients' quiet moments, and finally, all the sports equipment. She removed everything but life vests and foul-weather gear. By the time she finished, she had almost filled the floor of the office with it. Once again, she would have to call the secondhand dealer.

She pulled a soft cloth out of a box of cleaning materials and spread polish on the brass fittings. That, as well as cleaning the heads and galley, would keep her occupied.

As she worked—her hands and arms busy with the physical labor, her imagination playing every word, every look, every gesture that would signal her love to Gary—she lost track of time. Eventually, though, it began to seem as if the sea had become very choppy. She was swaying from side to side, until finally the motion affected her and she felt seasick, something which usually never bothered her. She had been kneeling next to the bunk in the small guest stateroom, rubbing furniture oil on the wooden base, and wondered if standing up would alleviate the symptoms. Perhaps she should leave that stateroom—it was always more uncomfortable any-way, being so much smaller. But trying to rise, she found it awkward getting her balance. Halfway up she fell back-ward, bruising her back against the edge of the built-in chest of drawers.

"Gary!" she yelled, "what's going on out there?"

There was no answer from topside. She managed to sit up and saw that only a faint light came through the porthole, as if it were twilight already. But that couldn't be. She hadn't been working that long. Bracing herself against the unpleasant roll, she struggled to her feet and managed to get out of the room and into the passage-way. The door banged shut behind her. Suddenly she noticed groans and creaks she had never heard before.

Up in the saloon, she discovered the drawers of the built-in tables had slid open. Fleetingly, she imagined what it would have been like in there had she not re-moved almost everything that wasn't tied down the day before. She left the gaping drawers as they were and made her way aft, but the hatch seemed jammed. Had it slammed shut with the force of the rocking motion or had Gary closed it? Whichever it was, it would not open for her. She banged on it furiously with the heel of her hand.

"Gary! Can you get this hatch open? I need some air."

There was no answer. She pulled at the handle with both hands, but couldn't make the hatch budge. She be-gan to feel both sick and claustrophobic. The *Southern Star* was tipped dangerously to port, as if there were no one at the wheel. A sudden jerk threw her across the sa-loon, banging her knee on the swivel chair. She clung to it for support until the boat righted itself somewhat, then managed to return to the hatchway just as the *Star* tipped in the other direction and sent her sprawling again. That time she put her hands out and braced herself before being tossed against another obstruction. Again her stomach heaved within her. She must get air or she would vomit.

She banged on the hatch with her fists, and finally, at last, Gary came. When his face appeared in the opening, she said, "I'm getting sick. I can't stay down here any longer."

"You're safer below. We're in a storm, a norther."

"It's too late for northers," she answered, as if denying the pitch and roll of the vessel and her own queasiness. Then she realized she was screaming over the sound of the wind. A storm beat at them. She had heard her father speak of northers but had never been caught in one before.

No matter, she had to get out of the cabin. "Open the hatch. I've got to come up."

"Put a slicker on to protect yourself from this spray."

Gary slammed the hatch shut again, and she went to the foul-weather locker and pulled out a yellow oilcloth slicker and matching hat. By then, she was so nauseated she could hardly stand, but she forced herself to the ladder again and pounded once more on the hatch.

Gary opened it, snatched her through, and banged it shut again. A five-foot wave crashed over the rail, drenching her.

Holding onto each other tightly, they crossed the slippery deck to the bridge, where Gary unchained the wheel and took hold of it again. "Stay close to me," he shouted over the noise of the wind and crashing waves. "I don't want you going overboard."

She gave him a weak smile.

"I checked the weather reports before we started out. Rain was predicted, even a bit of a blow, but nothing like this. A storm can come up so suddenly down here, sometimes you just can't anticipate them."

"I'll be all right," she said, clinging to the back of the sea chair for support. "It never occurred to me that the weather could turn so dirty this time of year."

"Northers can come up unexpectedly, sometimes in April. Anyway, I really wish you'd go back below."

She saw the deep frown on his forehead, the tight set of his jaw. Was he really worried about her? Or was it just the storm?

Another wave slammed into the *Star*, sending Marilee to her knees. She felt the salt water soak at once into her jeans and trickle inside her deck shoes. She looked to the port side. They were inching through the highest seas she had ever seen, slipping on them like a toboggan in a turn. There was no sun or sky. They seemed to be in some dark gray cavern where wind drove them against their will.

Then, just as suddenly, they were not careening madly before the wind, but climbing. She grabbed the base of the sea chair and hung on, but the lift threatened to somersault her out of the wheelhouse and across the deck. Then she noticed that Gary had taken down the canopy over the stern. When had he done that? It looked barren without it. But she had no time to consider the appearance of the vessel. They were now at the peak of the wave and fell into the trough that followed. The force threw her body the opposite way, so that she wound up in a heap at Gary's feet.

He reached down for her and pulled her upright. "You have to listen to me. Get below. This might get worse."

The wind rose again, and she had to scream to hear herself. "I don't want to leave you." She almost added, "I love you," then and there, but he interrupted and she reminded herself this was not the time or place.

"Do as I say," he ordered. "I'll need all my concentration to keep us afloat. I don't want to have to worry about you too."

With that she gave in and made her way, hand over hand, to the hatch and pulled hard at the handle. The wind took her breath away, and another wave sent gallons of ice-cold water across the deck and over her legs. Finally, the bolt shot open and she scrambled below and slammed the hatch shut behind her.

It was like another world, with the deck blotting out most of the noise above. But with the closeness, her seasickness returned. She struggled out of the slicker, plunged down the ladder, and was sick in the aft toilet. After a moment, she felt better in spite of the motion of the ship and went back to the saloon. Huddled in one of the chairs, which swiveled crazily from time to time with the violence of the storm, she sat and thought of Gary.

The pilot house offered considerable protection, she told herself, and of course, there were safety hooks and lines that could be used. He would snap himself into those if necessary. He was an experienced sailor, after all. He was strong and agile too, with muscular arms and legs. The sight of him moments before had reminded her again how intensely masculine he was. How had she ever managed to refuse him at eighteen? What a fool she'd been.

The *Star* tilted to port and, in spite of her hold on the sides of the chair, she went sprawling across the floor again, this time bumping herself on the base of the table. Regaining her footing, she went below to the master stateroom. Lying down on the bare mattress of the double bunk, she fastened the safety belt across her waist. The tossing and rolling of the ship were worse down there, but she knew this was a necessity if she hoped to keep from bruising herself even more.

But thoughts of Gary refused to leave her mind. Not that she was really worried for his safety. It wasn't hurricane season. This couldn't be the worst storm that had ever hit the Bahamas. They were through the current and within a short distance of land. Should the *Star* go down—and that seemed too incredible to consider—there was always the dinghy. They could make it to land in that.

Another roll of the yacht threw her toward the edge of the bunk, and she clutched the side of the mattress. The *Star* righted itself again, maintaining her certainty that nothing would happen to them. They had to make it to Nassau safely so she could tell Gary she loved him. They had to.

Chapter Twenty-one

Another thirty minutes went by before the next roll of the vessel was noticeably less violent, almost normal, in fact. Marilee unstrapped the safety belt and scrambled from the bunk and up the steps, finding she could walk steadily.

The hatch opened at her touch and she stepped on deck. It was still wet and slippery, but the *Star* no longer tipped so dangerously. Even the sky was lighter. Far to port, she saw the black clouds scudding before the wind. The storm was moving on.

She joined Gary in the pilot house. He smiled at her, but remained standing, facing forward with his hands on the wheel.

She touched his arm and felt the corded muscle through the sleeve of his Windbreaker. She stared at his strong profile. This was right. Her resolution to bare her own feelings remained as strong as before. She said a silent, grateful prayer that they had survived the storm.

He turned toward her, as if reading her thoughts, and

released one hand from the wheel to put it around her shoulders and press her to his side in a comforting gesture. "We're approaching the harbor, and I need you to ready the anchors. In a few minutes we'll be docking in Nassau."

She looked out at the unmistakable contour of the harbor dead ahead of them. It wouldn't be long now. Their conversation only had to wait until after they had berthed and she had signed over the *Star* to the new owner.

As she worked, she tried to glean something positive from Gary's words, looks, and gestures that might signal his love. She had just finished coiling the stern line on the dock when he shut down the engines and strode out of the wheelhouse. She looked up and their gaze locked. Suddenly nervous, she nevertheless refused to allow it to weaken her determination. She knew, finally, how deeply her feelings for him ran. One way or another, she would have a clear-cut response from him. It was a risk she'd have to take.

"You just have time for your appointment," he said. "While you run over there, I'll arrange for a car to take us to the airport. Then we'll catch the flight back to Eleuthera. I'll meet you in front of Johnson's door in ten minutes."

As he pushed her gently along the way, her throat tightened. There was no point in trying to tell him now. It was all too obvious he couldn't wait to be rid of her. With blurry vision, she saw him stride down Bay Street. A strange thought surfaced. Why Bay Street? Surely he could have found a taxi closer.

She walked quickly to the address on the papers Mike had given her, willing herself to keep going, to make this last final gesture that would cut her ties to Eleuthera and her past. As she stopped in front of the building, something familiar nagged at her. It was the name. The name on the plate glass window read PARADISE ISLAND YACHTS, the very place Gary had stopped that other time in Nassau, when he had returned with the Jaguar he had borrowed from his friend.

She pushed the memory away and stepped inside. Mr. Johnson, a sandy-haired young man wearing reading glasses with black frames, handed her a stack of papers and she put her signature on what seemed like a dozen legal-sized forms. She supposed she ought to read them, but hoped she didn't need to. She could trust Mike. Besides, she had to finish in a hurry before the enormity of selling the *Southern Star* overwhelmed her.

Finally finished, she rose from the chair and headed for the door, fishing in her bag for a handkerchief to hide the tears that welled in her eyes.

"Here, wait a minute," Johnson said. "You forgot your copy of the papers." While she waited, he gathered the stack he had put to one side and inserted them in a long manila envelope.

She took it from him and tried to give him a smile, but her lips wanted to curl downward and she knew it hadn't been successful. She let him open the door for her and stepped out, her stomach muscles tight, her throat choked. Almost at once Gary clutched her elbow and pulled her along the sidewalk.

"It's all over," she told him, the words almost refusing to come. "The *Star* is gone." Soon he would be gone as well. She could hardly breathe. Was this what it felt like to have your heart break?

But Gary continued to guide her down the street, and he was smiling. How could he be so jolly at a time like this?

She stopped walking. The charade had to end right then. She took a deep breath, then blurted it out before she could think and perhaps stop herself. "Gary, I love you."

He came to a halt at her side, eyes wide.

"I want to be with you," she rattled on. "I don't care if you charter cruises. I don't care what you do—sweep docks or haul garbage—I want to be with you."

She hurried to say the rest before he could stop her. "You were right all along. There, I've said it. And if you tell me it's too late, well, it's what I deserve."

Gary said nothing, only kissed her quickly on top of her head and pulled her along the sidewalk. When he finally stopped walking, she saw the same white Jaguar they'd used that other time waited at the curb, bright sunlight glinting off the polished surface. Gary opened the door and closed her in, then went around to the driver's side and started the engine.

But instead of driving toward the airport, he pulled into a parking lot, a grin still lighting his face. They were parked next to the same expensive restaurant that had provided a hamper of culinary delights the last time they were in Nassau.

"I thought we'd get a picnic lunch."

A picnic lunch? She was dying and he was thinking

of food. "Gary, listen to me. I love you. You told me that night on board the *Star* that I'd admit it before the cruise was over. Well, I didn't then, but I am now."

He stared at her but didn't interrupt.

"You were right about everything: why I never married, why I needed to see you again, why we were meant for each other." She stopped, realizing what his silence must mean. "I know you no longer love me. How could you, after what I did eight years ago? But I had to tell you, anyway."

He only smiled at her.

Through a flood of tears she reached for the door handle. She had to get away. She'd find a taxi to take her to the airport.

Gary caught her before she could exit the car. "Hold on just a minute." He pulled the envelope out of her hand and reached inside for one of the papers. He held it out to her, showed her a signature. Not hers, someone else's. Then, through blurred vision, the letters formed themselves into a recognizable name. Gary Pritchard.

"I don't understand."

"Look." He pointed to printing under the signature. "It says *Buyer*. That's me. Paradise Island Yachts belongs to me. And my partner Steve Johnson. But I'm buying the *Star* myself. No one else will ever have her."

"Paradise Island Yachts? Is that the name of your charter business?"

"No, I haven't done that in years. After you left me and I got over my self-destruct mode, I went back to school to learn marine architecture. I design and build yachts now. I really enjoy it as much as I once did sailing in them. And," he added, "it requires far less of my time and is a lot more lucrative." He grinned. "So I can afford to pay top dollar for the *Star.*"

"Gary," she repeated, the information beginning to connect in her mind, "Why? Tell me why you're doing this?" A sudden thought disturbed her. "I don't want you buying my way out of trouble. I can take care of myself."

"I know you can, but I don't want you to this time. The *Star* is my wedding present to you. That is, if you'll marry me." His hand gently brushed her hair.

"Did you say wedding present?" He did love her.

"I did. I couldn't tell you until now, but remember how upset you were when the Clarks decided not to buy the *Star?* I sabotaged the deal so I could buy her myself."

His words penetrated slowly. "Then you really were guilty? You weren't just covering up for Mike?" Another thought. "But we hadn't even started the cruise then. How did you know you'd even want to marry me?"

"I didn't know your feelings, but I did know mine. And when you came to my house that day to ask me to captain her, I decided that I had to try to get you back. We had to take that cruise together so I could find out, once and for all, if you still loved me." He twisted in the bucket seat and his other arm slid around her waist, bringing her close.

"But you didn't—" Before she could say more, he crushed her against his chest and his mouth claimed hers with a passion that was both familiar and welcome.

She gave herself up to the moment, holding him

tightly and repeating over and over to herself while his lips clung to hers, *he loves me, he loves me.* Her heart bounced and fluttered insanely.

At last he broke the kiss. He pressed a button and the convertible top whirred into action, lifting the canvas over their heads to blot out the stares of the passersby.

"Gary," she breathed, "why didn't you tell me how you felt the other day? I thought you didn't care if I left."

"Not care? I cared more than I can ever tell you. I never stopped loving you, Lee, or hoping that some day we'd find each other again. And then my most desired miracle came true. I hoped you were ready for me at last, but even then I couldn't be sure. I wanted to hear you say it, but even if you hadn't, by this time I was prepared to propose to you again."

"I didn't know it then, but—"

"We both knew it that day in Nassau."

"Oh, yes." She felt her heart expand at the very thought of it.

"But I didn't dare push or pressure you after we returned. You ran from me once before. How could I be sure that wouldn't happen again?" He paused for a moment. "And as soon as we docked, Howard showed up."

"But that didn't seem to bother you."

"If you knew how I really felt, you'd nominate me for an Oscar. I was terrified. And this time, I knew if you left, I'd have lost you for good."

She stroked the side of his face and touched his dark hair with her finger. "I never loved Howard. I think I must have come to that conclusion the moment I saw you again."

"I had to be certain you knew what you wanted." He kissed her cheeks, her lips, then drew back and looked deeply into her eyes.

"Oh, Gary, I hurt you once, very badly," she said. "I want to make it up to you, if you'll let me."

"We'll have the rest of our lives for that." He put his arms around her and held her tightly. "I want you to share my life forever."

Marilee looked up into his face and saw the love she had yearned for written there. "I'll gladly share your life. I love you, Gary. I don't care what you do, so long as I can do it with you."

"That's all I needed to hear. And now, Miss Shaw, I'm going to ask you for the last time: Will you marry me?"

She threw herself against him, her voice so choked she wasn't certain he understood her single word. "Yes."

His kiss gave unmistakable proof he heard her plainly.

Humphrey, Phyllis A.
Southern Star

FEB   2011